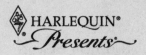

HARLEQUIN®
Presents~

Take a look at our books for September!

A marriage ended or a marriage mended? Kayla has been bought back by her estranged husband, billionaire Duardo Alvarez, in Helen Bianchin's scorcher *Purchased by the Billionaire*. Bedded for revenge or wedded for passion? Freya has made the mistake of hiding the existence of Italian Enrico Ranieri's little son, and she must make amends as his convenient wife in Michelle Reid's torrid tale *The Ranieri Bride*. Is revenge sweet? Greek tycoon Christos Carides certainly thinks so when he seduces Becca Summer in Kim Lawrence's sizzling story, *The Carides Pregnancy*. But for how long? Out for the count? Italian aristocrat Alessio Ramontella certainly thinks he's KO'd innocent English beauty Laura, but will she actually succumb to his ruthless seduction? Find out in *The Count's Blackmail Bargain* by Sara Craven. Meantime, Carol Marinelli's mixing business with intense pleasure in her new UNCUT novel, *Taken for His Pleasure*. It's a gold band of blackmail for temporary bride Maddison as she's forced to marry wealthy Greek Demetrius Papasakis in *The Greek's Convenient Wife* by Melanie Milburne. Mistress material? Nora Lang doesn't think she's got what it takes in Susan Napier's *Mistress for a Weekend*. But tycoon Blake MacLeod thinks Nora definitely has something special—confidential information. And he'll keep her in his bed to prevent her giving it away. Finally, an ultimatum...*The Marriage Ultimatum* by Helen Brooks. It's Carter Blake's only option when Liberty refuses to let him take her.

Harlequin Presents®

ITALIAN HUSBANDS

They're tall, dark—and ready to marry!

If you love marriage-of-convenience stories that ignite into marriages of passion, then look no further. We've got the heroes you love to read about and the women who tame them.

Watch for more exciting tales of romance, Italian-style!

Available only from Harlequin Presents®!

Sara Craven

THE COUNT'S BLACKMAIL BARGAIN

ITALIAN HUSBANDS

HARLEQUIN®

TORONTO • NEW YORK • LONDON
AMSTERDAM • PARIS • SYDNEY • HAMBURG
STOCKHOLM • ATHENS • TOKYO • MILAN • MADRID
PRAGUE • WARSAW • BUDAPEST • AUCKLAND

ISBN-13: 978-0-373-12567-8
ISBN-10:   0-373-12567-4

THE COUNT'S BLACKMAIL BARGAIN

First North American Publication 2006.

Copyright © 2005 by Sara Craven.

All about the author...
Sara Craven

SARA CRAVEN was born in South Devon, and
grew up surrounded by books in a house by the
sea. After leaving grammar school she worked
as a local journalist, covering everything from
flower shows to murders. She started writing for
Harlequin in 1975. Sara Craven has appeared as a
contestant on the U.K. Channel Four game show
Fifteen to One and in 1997 won the title
of Television Mastermind of Great Britain.

Sara shares her Somerset home with a West
Highland white terrier called Berlie Wooster,
several thousand books and an amazing video
and DVD collection.

When she's not writing, she likes to travel in
Europe, particularly Greece and Italy. She loves
music, theater, cooking and eating in good
restaurants, but reading will always be her
greatest passion.

Since the birth of her twin grandchildren in
New York City, she has become a regular visitor
to the Big Apple.

CHAPTER ONE

IT WAS a warm, golden morning in Rome, so how in the name of God was the city in the apparent grip of a small earthquake?

The noble Conte Alessio Ramontella lifted his aching head from the pillow, and, groaning faintly from the effort, attempted to focus his eyes. True, the bed looked like a disaster area, but the room was not moving, and the severe pounding, which he'd assumed was the noise of buildings collapsing nearby, seemed to be coming instead from the direction of his bedroom door.

And the agitated shouting he could hear was not emanating from some buried victim either, but could be recognised as the voice of his manservant Giorgio urging him to wake up.

Using small, economical movements that would not disturb the blonde, naked beauty still slumbering beside him, or increase the pressure from his hangover, Alessio got up from the bed, and extracted his robe from the tangle of discarded clothing on the floor, before treading across the marble-tiled floor to the door.

He pulled the garment round him, and opened the door an inch or two.

'This is not a working day,' he informed the anxious face outside. 'Am I to be allowed no peace?'

'Forgive me, *Eccellenza*.' Giorgio wrung his hands. 'For the world I would not have disturbed you. But it is your aunt, the Signora Vicente.'

There was an ominous pause, then: 'Here?' Alessio bit out the word.

'On her way,' Giorgio admitted nervously. 'She telephoned to announce her intention to visit you.'

Alessio swore softly. 'Didn't you have enough wit to say I was away?' he demanded.

7

'Of course, *Eccellenza*.' Giorgio spoke with real sorrow. 'But regrettably she did not believe me.'

Alessio swore again more fluently. 'How long have I got?'

'That will depend on the traffic, *signore*, but I think we must count in minutes.' He added reproachfully, 'I have been knocking and knocking...'

With another groan, Alessio forced himself into action. 'Get a cab for my guest,' he ordered. 'Tell the driver to come to the rear entrance, and to be quick about it. This is an emergency. Then prepare coffee for the *Signora*, and some of the little almond biscuits that she likes.'

He shut the door, and went back to the bed, his hangover eclipsed by more pressing concerns. He looked down at all the smooth, tanned loveliness displayed for his delectation, and his mouth tightened.

Dio, what a fool he'd been to break his own cardinal rule, and allow her to stay the night.

I must have been more drunk than I thought, he told himself cynically, then bent over her, giving one rounded shoulder a firm shake.

Impossibly long lashes lifted slowly, and she gave him a sleepy smile. 'Alessio, *tesoro mio*, why aren't you still in bed?' She reached up, twining coaxing arms round his neck to draw him down to her, but he swiftly detached the clinging hands and stepped back.

'Vittoria, you have to go, and quickly too.'

She pouted charmingly. 'But how ungallant of you, *caro*. I told you, Fabrizio is visiting his witch of a mother, and will not be back until this evening at the earliest. So we have all the time in the world.'

'An enchanting thought,' Alessio said levelly. 'But, sadly, there is no time to pursue it.'

She stretched voluptuously, her smile widening. 'But how can I leave, *mi amore*, when I have nothing to wear? You won all my clothes at cards last night, so what am I to do? It was, after all, a debt of honour,' she added throatily.

Alessio tried to control his growing impatience. 'Consider it cancelled. I cheated.'

She hunched a shoulder. 'Then you will have to fetch my clothes for me—from the *salotto* where I took them off. Unless you wish me to win them back, during another game of cards.'

This, thought Alessio, was not the time to be sultry.

His smile was almost a snarl. 'And how, precisely, *bella mia*, will you explain your presence, also your state of undress, to my aunt Lucrezia, who counts Fabrizio's mother among her closest cronies?'

Vittoria gave a startled cry and sat up, belatedly grabbing at the sheet. '*Madonna*—you cannot mean it. Promise me she is not here?'

'Not quite, but due imminently,' Alessio warned, his tone grim.

'*Dio mio.*' Her voice was a wail. 'Alessio—do something. I must get out of here. You have to save me.'

There was another knock at the door, which opened a crack to admit Giorgio's discreet arm holding out a handful of female clothing. His voice was urgent. 'The taxi has arrived, *Eccellenza*.'

'*Un momento.*' Alessio strode over and took the clothes, tossing them deftly to Vittoria who was already running frantically to the bathroom, her nakedness suddenly ungainly.

He paused, watching her disappear, then gave a mental shrug. Last night she'd been an entertaining and inventive companion, but daylight and danger had dissipated her appeal. There would be no more cards, or any other games with the beautiful Vittoria Montecorvo. In fact, he thought, frowning, it might be wiser, for the future, to avoid discontented wives altogether. The only real advantage of such affairs was not being expected to propose marriage, he told himself cynically.

He retrieved his underwear from the pile of discarded evening clothes beside the bed, then went into his dressing room, finding and shrugging on a pair of cream denim trousers and a black polo shirt. As he emerged, thrusting his bare feet into loafers, Vittoria was waiting, dressed but distraught.

'Alessio.' She hurled herself at him. 'When shall I see you again?'

The honest reply would be, 'Never,' but that would also be unkind.

'Perhaps this narrow escape is a warning to us, *cara mia*,' he returned guardedly. 'We shall have to be very careful.'

'But I am not sure I can bear it.' Her voice throbbed a little. 'Not now that we have found each other, *angelo mio*.'

Alessio suppressed a cynical smile. He knew who his predecessor had been. Was sure that his successor was already lined up. Vittoria was a rich man's beautiful daughter married to another rich man, who was all too easy to fool.

She was spoiled, predatory and bored, as, indeed, he was himself.

Maybe that had been the initial attraction between them, he thought, with an inner grimace. Like calling to like.

Suddenly he felt jaded and restless. The heat of Rome, the noise of the traffic seemed to press upon him, stifling him. He found himself thinking of windswept crags where clouds drifted. He longed to breathe the dark, earthy scents of the forests that clothed the lower slopes, and wake in the night to moonlit silence.

He needed, he thought, to distance himself.

And he could have all that, and more. After all, he was overdue for a vacation. Some re-scheduling at the bank, and he could be gone, he told himself as Vittoria pressed herself against him, murmuring seductively.

He wanted her out of the *appartamento*, too, he thought grimly, and realised he would have felt the same even if he hadn't been threatened by a visit from his aunt.

Gently but firmly, he edged her out of the bedroom, and along the wide passage to where Giorgio was waiting, his face expressionless, just as the entrance bell jangled discordantly at the other end of the flat.

'I'll get that. You take the *signora* to her cab.' Alessio freed himself from the clutching, crimson-tipped fingers, murmuring that of course he would think of her, would call her—but only if he felt it was safe.

He paused to watch her leaving, her parting glance both suspicious and disconsolate, then drew a deep breath of thanksgiving, raking the hair she'd so playfully dishevelled back from his face with impatient fingers.

The bell rang again, imperative in its summons, and Alessio knew he could hardly delay his response any longer. Sighing, he went to confront the enemy at the gates.

'Zia Lucrezia,' he greeted the tall, grey-haired woman waiting on his doorstep, her elegant shoe beating a tattoo against the stone. 'What a charming surprise.'

Her glance was minatory as she swept past him. 'Don't be a hypocrite, Alessio. It does not become you. I was not expecting to be welcome.' She paused for a moment, listening to the distant sound of a car starting up, and the rear door closing with a clang. 'Ah, so your other visitor has safely made her escape,' she added with a sour smile. 'I regret spoiling your plans for the day, nephew.'

He said gently, 'I rarely make plans, my dear aunt. I prefer to wait and see what delights the day offers.' He escorted her into the *salotto*, one swift, sweeping glance assuring him that it had been restored to its usual pristine condition. The tell-tale wineglasses had been removed, together with the empty bottles, and the *grappa* that had followed had also been put away. As had the scattered cards from last night's impromptu session of strip poker.

And the windows to the balcony stood innocently open to admit the morning sun, and dispel any lingering traces of alcohol fumes, and Vittoria's rather heavy perfume.

Making a mental note to increase Giorgio's salary, he conducted the Signora to a sofa, and seated himself in the chair opposite.

'To what do I owe the pleasure of seeing you, Zia Lucrezia?'

She was silent for a moment, then she said curtly, 'I wish to speak to you about Paolo.'

He looked across at her in frank surprise. Giorgio's arrival with the tall silver pot of coffee, and the ensuing ritual of pouring the coffee and handing the tiny sweet biscuits, gave him a chance to gather his thoughts.

When they were alone again, he said softly, 'You amaze me, *cara Zia*. I am hardly in a position to offer advice. You have always allowed me to understand that my example to your only son is an abomination.'

'Don't pretend to be a fool,' the Signora said shortly. 'Of course, I don't want advice.' She hesitated again. 'However, I do find that I need your practical assistance in a small matter.'

Alessio swallowed some coffee. 'I hope this is not a request to transfer Paolo back to Rome. I gather he is making progress in London.'

'That,' said Paolo's mother glacially, 'is a matter of opinion. And, anyway, he is returning to Rome quite soon, to spend his vacation with me.'

Alessio's eyes narrowed slightly. 'The idea doesn't appeal to you? Yet I remember you complaining to me when we met at Princess Dorelli's reception that you didn't see him often enough.'

There was another, longer silence, then the Signora said, as if the words were being wrung out of her, 'He is not coming alone.'

Alessio shrugged. 'Well, why should he?' he countered. 'Let me remind you, dear aunt, that my cousin is no longer a boy.'

'Precisely.' The Signora poured herself more coffee. 'He is old enough, in fact, to be a husband. And let me remind *you*, Alessio, that it has always been the intention of both families that Paolo should marry Beatrice Manzone.'

Alessio's brows snapped together. 'I know there was some such plan when they were children,' he admitted slowly. 'But now—now they are adults, and—things change. People change.'

She looked back at him stonily. 'Except for you, it seems, my dear nephew. You remain—unregenerate, with your boats and your fast cars. With your gambling and your womanising.'

He said gently, '*Mea culpa*, Zia Lucrezia, but we are not here to discuss my manifold faults.' He paused. 'So, Paolo has a girl-friend. It's hardly a mortal sin, and, anyway, to my certain knowl-edge, she is not the first. He will probably have many more before he decides to settle down. So, what is the problem?'

'Signor Manzone is an old friend,' said the Signora. 'Naturally, he wishes his daughter's future to be settled. And soon.'

'And is this what Beatrice herself wants?'

'She and my Paolo grew up together. She has adored him all her life.'

Alessio shrugged again. 'Then maybe she'll be prepared to wait until he has finished sowing his wild oats,' he returned in-differently.

'Hmm.' The Signora's tone was icy. 'Then it is fortunate she is not waiting for you.'

'Fortunate for us both,' Alessio said gently. 'The Signorina Manzone is infinitely too sweet for my taste.'

'I am relieved to hear it. I did not know you bothered to dis-criminate between one foolish young woman and the next.'

As so often when he talked to his aunt, Alessio could feel his jaw clenching. He kept his voice even. 'Perhaps you should re-member, *Zia*, that my father, your own brother, was far from a saint until he married my mother. Nonna Ramontella often told me she wore out her knees, praying for him.' *And for you*, he added silently.

'What a pity your grandmother is no longer here to perform the same service for you.' There was a pause, and, when she spoke again, the Signora's voice was slightly less acerbic. 'But we should not quarrel, Alessio. Your life is your own, whereas Paolo has—obligations, which he must be made to recognise. Therefore this—*relazione amorosa* of his must end, *quanta prima tanto meglio*.'

Alessio frowned again. 'But sooner may not be better for Paolo,' he pointed out. 'They may be genuinely in love. After all, this is the twenty-first century, not the fifteenth.'

The Signora waved a dismissive hand. 'The girl is completely unsuitable. Some English *sciattona* that he met in a bar in

London,' she added with distaste. 'From what I have gleaned from my fool of a son, she has neither family nor money.'

'Whereas Beatrice Manzone has both, of course,' Alessio said drily. 'Especially money.'

'That may not weigh with you,' the Signora said with angry energy. 'But it matters very much to Paolo.'

'Unless I break my neck playing polo,' Alessio drawled. 'Which would make him my heir, of course. My preoccupation with dangerous sports should please you, Zia Lucrezia. It opens up all kinds of possibilities.'

She gave him a fulminating look. 'Which we need not consider. You will, of course, remember in due course what you owe to your family, and provide yourself with a wife and family.

'As matters stand, you are the chairman of the Arleschi Bank. He is only an employee. He cannot afford to marry some pretty nobody.'

'So, she's pretty,' Alessio mused. 'But then she would have to be, if she has no money. And Paolo has Ramontella blood in his veins, so she may even be a beauty—this...?'

'Laura,' the Signora articulated coldly. 'Laura Mason.'

'Laura.' He repeated the name softly. 'The name of the girl that Petrarch saw in church and loved for the rest of his life.' He grinned at his aunt. 'I hope that isn't an omen.'

'Well,' the Signora said softly, 'I depend on you, my dear Alessio, to make certain it is not.'

'You expect me to preach to my cousin about family duty?' He laughed. 'I don't think he'd listen.'

'I wish you to do more than talk. I wish you to bring Paolo's little romance to an end.'

His brows lifted. 'And how am I supposed to do that?'

'Quite easily, *caro mio*.' She gave him a flat smile. 'You will seduce her, and make sure he knows of it.'

Alessio came out of his chair in one lithe, angry movement. 'Are you insane?'

'I am simply being practical,' his aunt returned. 'Requesting that you put your dubious talents with women to some useful purpose.'

'Useful!' He was almost choking on his rage. '*Dio mio*, how dare you insult me by suggesting such a thing? Imagine that I would be willing even for one moment...' He flung away from her. Walked to the window, gazed down into the street below with unseeing eyes, then turned back, his face inimical. 'No,' he said. 'And again—no. Never.'

'You disappoint me,' the Signora said almost blandly. 'I hoped you would regard it as—an interesting challenge.'

'On the contrary,' he said. 'I am disgusted—nauseated by such a proposal.' He took a deep breath. 'And from you of all people. You—astound me.'

She regarded him calmly. 'What exactly are your objections?'

He spread his hands in baffled fury. 'Where shall I begin? The girl is a complete stranger to me.'

'But so, at first, are all the women who share your bed.' She paused. 'For example, *mio caro*, how long have you known Vittoria Montecorvo, whose hasty departure just now I almost interrupted?'

Their eyes met, locked in a long taut, silence. Eventually, he said, 'I did not realise you took such a close interest in my personal life.'

'Under normal circumstances, I would not, I assure you. But in this instance, I need your—co-operation.'

Alessio said slowly, 'At any moment, I am going to wake up, and find this is all a bad dream.' He came back to his chair. Sat. 'I have other objections. Do you wish to hear them?'

'As you wish.'

He leaned forward, the dark face intense. 'This romance of Paolo's may just be a passing fancy. Why not let it run its course?'

'Because Federico Manzone wishes my son's engagement to Beatrice to be made official. Any more delay would displease him.'

'And would that be such a disaster?'

'Yes,' his aunt said. 'It would. I have entered into certain—accommodations with Signor Manzone, on the strict understanding that this marriage would soon be taking place. Repayment would be—highly inconvenient.'

'*Santa Maria.*' Alessio slammed a clenched fist into the palm of his other hand. Of course, he thought. He should have guessed as much.

The Signora's late husband had come from an old but relatively impoverished family, but, in spite of that, her spending habits had always been legendary. He could remember stern family conferences on the subject when he was a boy.

And age, it seemed, had not taught her discretion.

Groaning inwardly, he said, 'Then why not allow me to settle these debts for you, and let Paolo live his life?'

There was a sudden gleam of humour in her still-handsome face. 'I am not a welcome client at the bank, Alessio, so are you inviting me to become your private pensioner? Your poor father would turn in his grave. Besides, the lawyers would never allow it. And Federico has assured me very discreetly that, once our families are joined, he will make permanent arrangements for me. He is all generosity.'

'Then why not change the plan?' Alessio said with sudden inspiration. 'You're a widow. He's a widower. Why don't you marry him yourself, and let the next generation find their own way to happiness?'

'As you yourself are doing?' The acid was back. 'Perhaps we could have a double wedding, *mio caro*. I am sure honour will demand you ask the lovely Vittoria to be your wife, when her husband divorces her for adultery. After all, it will make a hideous scandal.'

Their glances met again and clashed, steel against steel.

He said steadily, 'I was not aware that Fabrizio had any such plans for Vittoria.'

'Not yet, certainly,' the Signora said silkily. 'But if he or my good friend Camilla, his mother, should discover in some unfortunate way that you have planted horns on him, then that might change.'

Eventually, Alessio sighed, lifting a shoulder in a resigned shrug. 'I have seriously underestimated you, Zia Lucrezia. I did not realise how totally unscrupulous you could be.'

'A family trait,' said the Signora. 'But desperate situations call for desperate measures.'

'But, you must still consider this,' Alessio went on. 'Even if his affair with the English girl is terminated, there is no guarantee that Paolo will marry Beatrice. He may still choose to look elsewhere. He might even find another rich girl. How will you prevent that?' He gave her a thin smile. 'Or have you some scheme to blackmail him into co-operation too?'

'You speak as if he has never cared for Beatrice.' His aunt spoke calmly. 'This is not true. And, once his disillusion with his English fancy is complete, I know he will realise where his best interests lie, and turn to her again. And they will be happy together. I am sure of it.'

Alessio sent her a look of pure exasperation. 'How simple you make it sound. You pull the strings, and the puppets dance. But there are still things you have not taken into account. For one thing, how will I meet this girl?'

'I have thought of that. I shall tell Paolo that I have workmen at my house in Tuscany putting in a new heating system, so cannot receive guests. Instead, I have accepted a kind invitation from you for us all to stay at the Villa Diana.'

He snorted. 'And he will believe you?'

She shrugged. 'He has no choice. And I shall make sure you have the opportunity to be alone with the girl. The rest is up to you.' She paused. 'You may not even be called on to make the ultimate sacrifice, *caro*. It might be enough for Paolo to discover you kissing her.'

He said patiently, 'Zia Lucrezia, has it occurred to you that this—Laura—may be truly in love with Paolo, and nothing will persuade her to even a marginal betrayal?'

He paused, his mouth twisting. 'Besides, and more importantly, you have overlooked the fact that she may not find me attractive.'

'*Caro* Alessio,' the Signora purred. 'Let us have no false modesty. It has been often said that if you had smiled at Juliet, she would have left Romeo. Like your other deluded victims, Laura will find you irresistible.'

'*Davvero?*' Alessio asked ironically. 'I hope she slaps my face.' He looked down at his hand, studying the crest on the signet ring he wore. 'And afterwards—if I succeed in this contemptible ploy? I would not blame Paolo if he refused to speak to me again.'

'At first, perhaps, he may be resentful. But in time, he will thank you.' She rose. 'They will be arriving next week. I hope this will not be a problem for you?'

He got to his feet too, his mouth curling. He walked over to her, took her hand and bowed over it. 'I shall count the hours.'

'Sarcasm, *mio caro*, does not become you.' She studied him for a moment. 'Like your father, Alessio, you are formidable when you are angry.' She patted his cheek. 'I hope you're in a better mood when you finally encounter this English girl, or I shall almost feel sorry for her.'

He gave her a hard, unsmiling look. 'Don't concern yourself for her, Zia Lucrezia. I will do my best to send her home with a beautiful memory.'

'Ah,' she said. 'Now I really do feel sorry for her.' And was gone.

Alone, Alessio went to a side table, and poured himself a whisky. He rarely drank in the daytime, but this was like no other day since the beginning of the world.

What the devil was Paolo thinking of—bringing his little *ragazza* within a hundred miles of his mother? If he gave a damn about her, he would keep them well apart.

And if I had an atom of decency, Alessio thought grimly, I would call him, and say so.

But he couldn't risk it. Zia Lucrezia had more than her full share of the Ramontella ruthlessness, as he should have remembered, and would not hesitate to carry out her veiled threat about his ill-advised interlude with Vittoria. And the fall-out would, as she'd predicted, be both unpleasant and spectacular.

Laura, he repeated to himself meditatively. Well, at least she had a charming name. If she had a body to match, then his task might not seem so impossible.

He raised his glass. '*Salute*, Laura,' he said with cynical emphasis. '*E buona fortuna.*' He added softly, 'I think you will need it.'

CHAPTER TWO

'WELL, it all sounds iffy to me,' said Gaynor. 'Think about it. You've cancelled your South of France holiday with Steve because you didn't like the sleeping arrangements, yet now you're off to Italy with someone you hardly know. It doesn't make any sense.'

Laura sighed. 'Not when you put it like that, certainly. But it truly isn't what you think. I'm getting a free trip to Tuscany for two weeks, plus a cash bonus, and all I have to do is look as if I'm madly in love.'

'It can't be that simple,' Gaynor said darkly. 'Nothing ever is. I mean, have you ever *been* madly in love? You certainly weren't with Steve or you wouldn't have quibbled about sharing a room with him,' she added candidly.

Laura flushed. 'I suppose I thought I was—or that I might be, given time. After all, we've only been seeing each other for two months. Hardly a basis for that kind of commitment.'

'Well, not everyone would agree with you there,' Gaynor said drily.

'I know.' Laura paused in her packing to sigh again. 'I'm a freak—a throwback. I admit it. But if and when I have sex with a man, I want it to be based on love and respect, and a shared future. Not because double rooms are cheaper than singles.'

'And what kind of room is this Paolo Vicente offering?'

'All very respectable,' Laura assured her, tucking her only swimsuit into a corner of her case. 'We'll be staying with his mother at her country house, and she's a total dragon, it seems. Paolo says she'll probably lock me in at night.'

'And she has no idea that you're practically strangers?'

'No, that's the whole point. She's pushing him hard to get engaged to a girl he's known all his life, and he won't. He says

20

she's more like his younger sister than a future wife, and that I'm going to be his declaration of independence. A way of telling his mother that he's his own man, and quite capable of picking a bride for himself.'

'Isn't that like showing a red rag to a bull? Do you *want* to be caught in the middle of two warring factions?'

'I won't be. Paolo says, at worst, she'll treat me with icy politeness. And he's promised I won't see that much of her—that he'll take me out and about as much as possible.' Laura paused. 'It could even be fun,' she added doubtfully.

'Ever the optimist,' muttered Gaynor. 'How the hell did you ever become part of this gruesome twosome?'

Laura sighed again. 'He works for the Arleschi Bank. We pitched for their PR work a few weeks ago, and Carl took me along to the presentation. Paolo was there. Then, a fortnight ago, he came into the wine bar, and we recognised each other.' She wrinkled her nose. 'I'd just split with Steve, so I was feeling down, and Paolo was clearly fed up too. He stayed on after closing time, and we had a drink together, and started talking.

'He wanted to know why I was moonlighting in a wine bar when I was working for Harman Grace, so I told him about Mum being a widow, and Toby winning that scholarship to public school, but always needing extra stuff for school, plus this field trip in October.

'Then Paolo got very bitter about his mother, and the way she was trying to tie him down with this Beatrice. And, somehow, over a few glasses of wine, the whole scheme evolved.'

She shook her head. 'At first, I thought it was just the wine talking, but when he came back the following night to hammer out the details I discovered he was deadly serious. I also realised that the extra cash he was offering would pay for Toby's field trip, and compensate Steve for the extra hotel charges he's been emailing me about incessantly.'

'Charming,' said Gaynor.

Laura pulled a face. 'Well, I did let him down over the holiday, so I suppose he's entitled to feel sore.

'However, when push came to shove, I honestly couldn't af-

ford to turn Paolo down.' She sounded faintly dispirited, then
rallied. 'And, anyway, I've always wanted to go to Italy. Also it
may be my last chance of a proper holiday, before I seriously
start saving towards the Flat Fund.'

'I've already begun.' Gaynor gave a disparaging glance around
the cramped bedsit, a mirror-image of her own across the landing.
'There's an ugly rumour that Ma Hughes is all set to raise the
rents again. If we don't find our own place soon, we won't be
able to afford to move out. And Rachel from work is definitely
interested in joining us,' she added buoyantly. 'Apparently, living
at home is driving her crazy.'

  She got up from the bed, collecting up their used coffee-cups.
On her way to the communal kitchenette, she paused at the door.
'Honey, you are sure you can trust this Paolo? He won't suddenly
develop wandering hands when you're on your own with him?'

Laura laughed. 'I'm sure he won't. He likes voluptuous bru-
nettes, so I'm really not his type, and he certainly isn't mine,'
she added decisively. 'Although I admit he's good-looking.
Besides, I have his mother as chaperon, don't forget. And he tells
me she strongly disapproves of open displays of affection, so all
I really have to do is flutter my eyelashes occasionally.'

Laura gave a brisk nod. 'No, this is basically a business arrangement, and that's fine with me.'

Her smile widened. 'And I get to see Tuscany at last. Who
could ask for more?'

But as the plane began its descent towards Rome's Leonardo da
Vinci Airport she did not feel quite so euphoric about the situation, although she could not have fully explained why.

She had met up with Paolo the previous night to talk over final
details for the trip.

'If we're dating each other, then you need to know something
about me, *cara*, and my family,' he explained with perfect reason.

She'd already gathered that he occupied a fairly junior position
at the bank's London branch. What she hadn't expected to hear

was that he was related to the Italian aristocrat who was the Arleschi chairman.

'We are the poor side of the family,' he explained. He was smiling, but there was a touch of something like peevishness in his voice. 'Which is why my mother is so eager for me to marry Beatrice, of course. Her father is a very wealthy man, and she is his only child.'

'Of course,' Laura echoed. Who are these people? she wondered in frank amazement. And just what planet do they inhabit?

She thought of her mother struggling to make ends meet. Of herself, spending long evenings in the wine bar so that she could help towards her shy, clever brother having the marvellous education he deserved.

When Paolo used the term 'poor' so airily, he had no idea what it really meant.

Her throat tightened. She'd treated herself to some new clothes for the abortive French holiday, but they were all chain-store bought, with not a designer label among them.

She was going to stick out like the proverbial sore thumb in this exclusive little world she was about to join, however briefly. So, could she really make anyone believe that she and Paolo were seriously involved?

But perhaps this was precisely why he had chosen her, she thought unhappily. Because she was so screamingly unsuitable. Maybe this would provide exactly the leverage Paolo needed to escape from this enforced marriage.

'Anyone,' his mother might say, throwing up her hands in horrified surrender. 'Anyone but her!'

Well, she could live with that, because Paolo, in spite of his smoothly handsome looks and august connections, held no appeal for her. In fact, Laura decided critically, she wouldn't have him if he came served on toast with a garnish.

He was arrogant, she thought, and altogether too pleased with himself, and, although no one should be forced to marry someone they didn't love, on balance her sympathies lay with his would-be fiancée.

'I must insist on one thing,' she said. 'No mention of Harman Grace.'

'As you wish.' He shrugged. 'But why? They are a good company. You have nothing to be ashamed of by working for them.'

'I know that. But we're now the bank's official PR company in London. Your cousin must know that, and he'll recognise the name if it's mentioned. He may not appreciate the fact that you're supposedly dating someone who's almost an employee.'

'Don't disturb yourself, *cara*. I am nothing more than an employee myself. Besides, the chances of your meeting my cousin Alessio are slim. But Harman Grace shall remain a secret between us, if that's what you want.'

'Yes,' she said. 'I really do. Thank you.'

She was astonished to find that they were flying first class, proving that poverty was only relative, she thought grimly, declining the champagne she was automatically offered.

A couple of glasses of wine had got her into this mess. So, from now on she intended to keep a cool head.

She was also faintly disconcerted by Paolo's attempts to flirt with her. He kept bending towards her, his voice low and almost intimate as he spoke. And she didn't like his persistent touching either—her hair, her shoulder, the sleeve of her linen jacket.

Oh, God, she thought uneasily. Don't tell me Gaynor was right about him all along.

She was aware, with embarrassment, that the cabin staff were watching them, exchanging knowing looks.

'What are you doing?' she muttered, pulling her hand away as he tried to kiss each of her fingers.

He shrugged, not in the least discomposed. 'For every performance, there must be a rehearsal, no?'

'Definitely no,' Laura said tartly.

She was also disappointed to hear there'd been a slight change of plan. That instead of hiring a car at the airport and driving straight to Tuscany, they were first to join the Signora Vicente at her Rome apartment.

'But for how long?' she queried.

Paolo was unconcerned. 'Does it matter? It will give you a

chance to see *my* city before we bury ourselves in the country-side,' he told her. He gave a satisfied smile. 'Also, my mother employs a driver and a car for her journeys, so we shall travel in comfort.'

Laura felt she had no option but to force a smile of agreement. It's his trip, she thought resignedly. I'm just the hired help.

The Signora's residence was in the Aventine district, which Paolo told her was one of the city's more peaceful locations with many gardens and trees.

She occupied the first floor of a grand mansion, standing in its own grounds, and Laura took a deep, calming breath as they mounted the wide flight of marble stairs.

You've got your passport in your bag, she reminded herself silently. Also, your return ticket. All you have to do, if you really can't hack this, is turn and run.

When they reached the imposing double doors, Paolo rang the bell, and Laura swallowed as he took her hand in his with a reassuring nod.

It's only a couple of weeks, she thought. Not the rest of my life.

The door was opened by a plump elderly maid, who beamed at Paolo, ignoring Laura completely, then burst into a flood of incomprehensible Italian.

Laura found herself in a windowless hall, its only illumination coming from a central chandelier apparently equipped with low-wattage bulbs. The floor was tiled in dark marble, and a few pieces of heavy antique furniture and some oil paintings in ornate frames did little to lighten the atmosphere.

Then the maid flung open the door to the *salotto*, and sunlight struggled out, accompanied by a small hairy dog, yapping furiously and snarling round their ankles.

'Quiet, Caio,' Paolo ordered, and the dog backed off, although it continued its high-pitched barking, and growling. Laura liked dogs, and usually got on with them, but something told her that Caio was more likely to take a chunk out of her ankle than respond to any overtures she might make.

Paolo led her into the room. 'Call off your hound, *Mamma*,' he said. 'Or my Laura will think she is not welcome.'

'But I am always ready to receive your friends, *figlio mio*.' The Signora rose from a brocaded sofa, and offered her hand.

She was a tall woman, Laura saw, and had been handsome once rather than a beauty. But time had thinned her face and narrowed her mouth, and this, together with her piercing dark eyes, made her formidable. She wore black, and there were pearls round her neck, and in her ears.

'Signorina Mason, is it not so?' Her smile was vinegary as she absorbed Laura's shy response. 'You would like some tea, I think. Is that not the English habit?'

Laura lifted her chin. 'Now that I'm here, *signora*, perhaps I should learn a few Italian customs instead.'

The elegantly plucked brows lifted. 'You will hardly be here long enough to make it worthwhile, *signorina*—but as you wish.' She rang a bell for the maid, ordered coffee and cakes, then beckoned Paolo to join her on the sofa.

This, thought Laura, taking the seat opposite that she'd been waved towards, is going to be uphill all the way. And she was still inwardly flinching from 'my Laura'.

It was a beautiful room, high-ceilinged and well proportioned, but massively over-furnished for her taste. There were too many groups of hard-looking chairs, she thought, taking a covert glance around. And far too many spindly-legged tables crowded with knick-knacks. The windows were huge, and she longed to drag open the tall shutters that half-masked them and let in some proper light. But she supposed that would fade the draperies, and the expensive rugs on the parquet floor.

'I have some news for you, *mio caro*,' the Signora announced, after the maid had served coffee and some tiny, but frantically rich chocolate cakes. 'And also for the *signorina*, your companion. I regret that I cannot after all entertain you at my country home. It is occupied by workmen—so tedious, but unavoidable.'

Laura froze, her cup halfway to her lips. Were they going to spend the whole two weeks in this apartment? Oh, God, she thought, surely not. It might seem spacious enough, but she suspected that even a few days with the Signora would make it seem totally claustrophobic.

Paolo was looking less than pleased. 'But you knew we were coming, *Mamma*. And I promised Laura that she should see Tuscany.'

'Another time, perhaps,' the Signora said smoothly. 'This time she will have to be content with a corner of Umbria.' Her expression was bland. 'Your cousin Alessio has offered us the use of the Villa Diana at Besavoro.'

There was an astonished pause, then Paolo said slowly, 'Why should he do that?'

'*Mio caro.*' The Signora's voice held a hint of reproof. 'We are members of his family. His only living relatives.'

Paolo shrugged. 'Even so, it is not like him to be so obliging,' he countered. 'And, anyway, Besavoro is at the end of the world.' He spread his hands. 'Also, the Villa Diana is halfway up a mountain on the way to nowhere. It is hardly an adequate substitute.'

'I think Signorina Mason will find it charming.' Again the smile that did not reach her eyes. 'And not overrun by her own countrymen.' She turned to Laura. 'I understand that Tuscany has come to be known as Chiantishire. So amusing.'

'Has it?' Laura enquired with wooden untruthfulness. 'I didn't know.' Dear God, she thought. I'm going to be staying at a house owned by the chairman of the Arleschi Bank. This can't be happening.

'And Umbria is very beautiful,' the Signora continued. 'They call it the green heart of Italy, and there are many places to visit—Assisi—Perugia—San Sepulcro, the birthplace of the great Rafael. You will be spoiled for choice, *signorina*.'

Paolo cast a glance at the decorated ceiling. 'You call it a choice, *Mamma*?' he demanded. 'To risk our lives up and down that deathtrap of a road every time we want to go anywhere?' He shook his head. 'If anything happens to my cousin Alessio, and I inherit, then the Villa Diana will be for sale the next day.'

There was another lengthier pause. Then: 'You must forgive my son, *signorina*,' the Signora said silkily. 'In the heat of the moment, he does not always speak with wisdom. And, even if it is a little remote, the house is charming.'

'And Alessio?' Paolo demanded petulantly, clearly resenting the rebuke. 'At least he can't mean to use the house himself, if we are there. Or he never has in the past.' He snorted. 'Probably off chasing some skirt.'

'Dear boy, the offer was made, and I was glad to accept. I did not enquire into his own plans.'

Laura had been listening with a kind of horrified fascination. She thought, I should not be hearing this.

Aloud, she said quietly, 'Paolo—isn't there somewhere else we could stay? A hotel, perhaps.'

'In the height of the tourist season?' Paolo returned derisively. 'We would be fortunate to find a cellar. No, it will have to be my cousin's villa. And at least it will be cooler in the hills,' he added moodily. 'When do we leave?'

'I thought tomorrow,' said the Signora. She rose. 'You must be tired after the flight, Signorina Mason. I shall ask Maria to show you your room so that you may rest a little.'

And so you can give your son your unvarnished opinion of his latest acquisition, thought Laura. But then this was only what she'd been led to expect, she reminded herself. She supposed she should be grateful that the Signora hadn't made a hysterical scene and ordered her out of the apartment.

The bedroom allocated to her was on the small side, and the bed was narrow, and not particularly comfortable. She had been shown the bathroom—a daunting affair in marble the colour of rare beef, but she was glad to find that the still-unsmiling Maria had supplied a jug of hot water and a matching basin for the washstand in her room.

She took off her shoes and dress, and had a refreshing wash. The soap was scented with lavender, and she thought with faint self-derision that it was the first friendly thing she'd discovered so far in Rome.

She dried herself with the rather harsh linen towel, then stretched out on top of the bed with a sigh.

The regrets she'd experienced on the plane were multiplying

with every moment that passed. Back in London, Paolo had persuaded her that it would be easy. A spot of acting performed against a backdrop of some of Europe's most beautiful scenery. Almost a game, he'd argued. And she'd be paid for it.

Well, she was fast coming to the conclusion that no amount of cash was worth the hassle that the next two weeks seemed to promise. Although most of her concerns about Paolo's future behaviour were largely laid to rest. The Signora, she thought with wry amusement, would prove a more than adequate chaperon. And if she had been in love with him, she'd have been faced with a frustrating time.

Her head was beginning to ache, and she reached down to her bag by the side of the bed for the small pack of painkillers she'd included at the last minute, and the bottle of mineral water she'd bought at the airport. It was lukewarm now, but better than nothing, she thought as she swallowed a couple of the tablets, then turned onto her side, resolutely closing her eyes.

The deed was done. She was in Italy, even if it wasn't turning out to be a dream come true.

Whatever, she thought wearily. There was no turning back now.

Dinner that night was not an easy occasion. Paolo had announced plans to take Laura out for a meal, but the Signora had pointed out with steely insistence that this would be unwise, as they would be making an early start in the morning to avoid travelling in the full heat of the day.

So they ate in the formal dining room, at a table that would have accommodated three times their number with room to spare. It did not make for a relaxed atmosphere, and conversation was so stilted that Laura wished Paolo and his mother would just speak Italian to each other, and leave her out of the situation.

She realised, of course, that she was being grilled. Remembered too that she and Paolo had agreed to keep her actual personal details to a minimum. As far as the Signora was concerned, she was a girl who shared a flat with several others, and who enjoyed a good time. Someone, she hinted with a touch of coy-

ness, who had not allowed for the sudden entry of Mr Right into
her life. And she sent Paolo a languishing look.

And whatever slights and unpleasantness might come her way,
Laura knew she would always treasure the memory of the expression on the august lady's face as she absorbed that.

She had rehearsed the invented story of how and when she
and Paolo had met so often that she was word-perfect. After all,
she needed to give the impression that theirs was an established
relationship of at least two months' standing, which deserved to
be taken seriously, and might be ready to move on to the next
stage.

For Steve, she thought with wry regret, substitute Paolo.

She even managed to turn some of the Signora's more probing
queries into her background back on themselves by ingenuously
asking what Paolo had been like as a small boy, and whether
there were any childhood photographs of him that she could see.

She had to admit the food was delicious, although she'd had
little appetite for it. And when dinner was over they returned to
the *salotto*, and listened to music by Monteverdi.

And that, thought Laura, was by far the most pleasant part of
the evening, not just because her late father had loved the same
composer, but because conversation was kept to a minimum.

She was just beginning to relax when the Signora announced
in a tone that did not welcome opposition that it was time to
retire for the night.

Paolo wished her a very correct goodnight outside the *salotto*,
but when Laura, dressing-gown clad, returned from the bathroom, she found him waiting in her room.

She checked uneasily. 'What are you doing here?'

'I wished to speak to you in private.' The grin he sent her was
triumphant. 'You are completely brilliant, *carissima. Dio mio*,
you almost convinced me. And *Mamma* is in such a fury.' He
shook his head. 'I have just overheard her on the telephone, and
she was *incandescente*. She must be speaking to her old friend
Camilla Montecorvo, because she mentioned the name Vittoria
several times.'

'Does that mean something?' Laura felt suddenly tired, and more than a little bewildered.

'Vittoria is the *nuora*—the daughter-in-law—of Signora Montecorvo,' Paolo explained, his grin widening. 'She causes big problems, and *Mamma* has heard all about them. Always, she has been the one to give advice to Camilla. But now it is her turn to complain,' he added gleefully. 'And she insists that her friend must listen, and help her.'

He almost hugged himself. 'It is all going as I hoped.'

'I wish I could say the same.' Laura bit her lip.

'You are regretting Tuscany?' Paolo shrugged. 'It was an unwelcome surprise for me also. And Alessio has other houses he could have lent *Mamma* that are not as remote as Besavoro,' he added, grimacing. 'For instance, he has a place near Sorrento where he keeps his boat, but no doubt he will be using that himself. He would not choose to stay anywhere near *Mamma*, so calm yourself on that point.'

'You're not a very close family,' Laura commented.

'Alessio likes to go his own way. *Mamma* tries to interfere.' He shrugged again. 'Maybe he is hoping she will stray too far from the house, and be eaten by the wolves.'

Laura stared at him. 'You mean there are such things..actually running wild?' Her tone held a hollow note.

'Yes, and they are on the increase. And there are bears too.' He laughed at her expression. 'But they are mainly found in the national parks, and I promise you that they prefer orchards and beehives to humans.'

'How—reassuring.' Laura took a deep breath. 'But it's not just disappointment over Tuscany, Paolo. Or the thought of moving to some Italian safari park either.'

She gave him a steady look. 'We shouldn't have started this. If your mother's so genuinely upset, it isn't a game any longer. I feel we should rethink.'

'For me, it has never been a game.' Paolo smote himself on the chest. 'For me—it is my life! I need my mother to know that my future is my own affair, and that I will not be dictated to by her or anyone. And that I am not going to marry Beatrice

Manzone.' He lowered his voice. Made it coaxing. 'Laura—you promised you would help me. We have an agreement together. And it is going well. Just two weeks—that is all. Then you will be free. You will have had your Italian vacation, and also been paid. This is so easy for you.'

He dropped a hand on her shoulder, making her move restively. 'After all,' he went on persuasively, 'what can possibly happen in two short weeks? Tell me that.' He smiled at her, then moved to the door. 'I tell you there is nothing to worry about.' His voice was warm—reassuring. 'Nothing in the world.'

CHAPTER THREE

LAURA did not sleep well that night. She was constantly tossing and turning, disturbed by a series of fleeting, uneasy dreams. Or, she wondered as daylight imposed itself at last, was she simply troubled by finding herself under the roof of a woman who cordially detested her—and with no reprieve in sight?

It was no particular surprise to find that the early start to Besavoro did not transpire. The car arrived punctually with Giacomo, its uniformed chauffeur, and there the matter rested while the Signora, after a leisurely breakfast, issued a stream of contradictory orders, made telephone calls, and wrote a number of last minute notes to friends.

Laura had discovered to her dismay that Caio was to accompany them and more time was wasted while Maria hunted the apartment for the special collar and lead he wore on holiday, and the new cushioned basket specially bought for the trip.

By the time the luggage was finally put in the car, Paolo looked as if he was about to become a basket case himself, Laura thought without particular sympathy.

It was one of the most luxurious vehicles she'd ever travelled in, but, seated in the back with the Signora and her dog in the opposite corner, she found it impossible to relax.

She'd expected another barrage of questions, and steeled herself to fend them off, but it didn't happen. The Signora seemed lost in thought, and, apart from lifting his lip in the occasional silent snarl if Laura glanced at him, Caio seemed equally detached.

There were numerous stops along the way—comfort breaks for Caio featuring frequently. But there were also pauses to buy coffee, chilled mineral water, and, once, some excellent rolls crammed with ham and cheese, at the busy roadside service stations. The Signora did not deign to leave the car on these occasions, but Laura was glad to stretch her legs in spite of the heat outside the air-conditioned car.

Her back was beginning to ache with the tension of trying to remain unobtrusive, she realised wryly.

She'd chosen her thinnest outfit for the journey—a loose-fitting dress in fine cream cotton with cap sleeves and a modestly square neckline. She wore low-heeled tan sandals, and a broad brimmed linen hat that could be rolled up in her bag when she was in the car. Apart from the obligatory sunblock, she'd put nothing on her face but a shading of mascara on her lashes, and a touch of light coral lustre to her mouth.

She tried to comfort herself with the reflection that the Signora might loathe her, but she couldn't truthfully complain about her appearance. Still it seemed small consolation.

The car didn't really need air conditioning, she thought ruefully. Paolo's mother could have lowered the temperature to arctic proportions with one look. And the cost of her brother's school trip was rising by the minute. He'd better enjoy it, that's all, she muttered under her breath.

But as they drove into Umbria she found herself succumbing to the sheer beauty of the scenery around her, all other considerations taking second place. Everywhere she looked seemed to be composed of endless shades of green, and every hilltop seemed crowned with its own little town, clinging precariously to its rocky crag.

Half an hour later they reached Besavoro, which seemed to be hardly more than a large village on the bank of a river, which Paolo told her was a tributary of the Tiber. The central point was the square, where houses and shops huddled round a tall, ornate church. There was a market taking place, and the cramped space had to be negotiated with care.

Once free of the village, they began to climb quite steeply, taking a narrow road up the side of the valley. They passed the occasional house, but generally it was rugged terrain with a steep rocky incline leading up to heavy woodland on one side, and, on the other, protected only by a low wall, a stomach-churning drop down to the clustering roofs, and the river, now reduced to a silver thread, below them.

She remembered Paolo's comment about a death trap, and suppressed a shiver, thankful that Giacomo was such a good driver.

'We are nearly there, *signorina*.' To her surprise, Laura found herself being addressed by the Signora. The older woman was even smiling faintly. 'No doubt you are eager to see where you will be spending your little vacation. I hope it lives up to your expectations.'

Any overture, however slight, was welcome, and Laura responded. 'Has the house been in the family long?' she enquired politely.

'For generations, although it has been altered and extended over the years. At one time, it is said to have been a hermitage, a solitary place where monks who had sinned were sent to do penance.'

'I know how they feel,' Paolo commented over his shoulder. 'I am astonished that Alessio should waste even an hour in such a place. He has certainly never repented of anything in his life.'

His mother shrugged. 'He spent much of his childhood here. Perhaps it has happy memories for him.'

'He was never a child,' said Paolo. 'And his past is what happened yesterday—no more.' He leaned forward. 'Look, Laura *mia*. You can see the house now, if you look down a little through the trees.'

She caught a glimpse of pale rose stonework, and faded terracotta tiles, and caught her breath in sudden magic.

It was like an enchanted place, sleeping among the trees, she thought, and she was coming to break the spell. And she smiled to herself, knowing she was being utterly absurd.

Impossible to miss the sound of an approaching car in the clear air, Alessio thought. His unwanted guests were arriving.

Sighing irritably, he swung himself off the sun lounger, and reached for the elderly pair of white tennis shorts lying on the marble tiles beside him, reluctantly dragging them on. For the past few days, he'd revelled in freedom and isolation. Basked in his ability to swim in the pool and sunbathe beside it naked, knowing that Guillermo and Emilia who ran the villa for him would never intrude on his privacy.

Now his solitude had ended.

He thrust his feet into battered espadrilles, and began walking up through the terraced gardens to the house.

Up to the last minute, he'd prayed that this nightmare would never happen. That Paolo and his *ragazza* would quarrel, or that Zia Lucrezia would love her as a daughter on sight, and withdraw her objections. Anything—anything that would let him off this terrible hook.

But her phone call the previous night had destroyed any such hopes. She'd been almost hysterical, he remembered with distaste, railing that the girl was nothing more than a gold-digging tart, coarse and obvious, a woman of the lowest class. But clever in a crude way because she obviously intended to trap into marriage her poor Paolo, who did not realise the danger he was in.

At the same time, she'd made it very clear that her threat to expose his fleeting affair with Vittoria, if he did not keep his word, was all too real.

'I want the English girl destroyed,' she had hissed at him. 'Nothing less will do.'

Alessio had been tempted to reply that he would prefer to destroy Vittoria, who was proving embarrassingly tenacious, bombarding him with phone calls and little notes, apparently unaware that her voluptuously passionate body in no way compensated for her nuisance value.

If she continued to behave with such indiscretion, Fabrizio and his mother might well smell a rat, without any intervention from Zia Lucrezia, he told himself grimly.

He'd been thankful to escape from Rome, and Vittoria's constant badgering, to this private hideaway where he could remain *incomunicabile*. He hoped that, during his absence, she would find some other willing target for her libido, or he might ultimately have to be brutal with her. A thought that gave him no pleasure whatsoever.

And now he was faced with another, worse calamity. This

unknown, unwanted girl that he had somehow to entice from Paolo's bed into his own. Probably, he decided, after he'd deliberately made himself very, very drunk...

If I emerge alive from this mess, I shall take a vow of celibacy, he thought moodily.

Guillermo was already opening the heavy wooden entrance door, and Emilia was hovering anxiously. He knew that his instructions would have been minutely carried out, and that the arrangements and the food would be perfect. But visitors at the villa were still a rarity, and the servants were more accustomed to their employer's own brand of casual relaxation. Zia Lucrezia's presence would prove taxing for all of them.

He stepped out of the shadowy hall into the sunlight. The car had halted a few feet away, and the chauffeur was helping the Signora to alight, while Caio yapped crossly from her arms.

But Alessio's attention was immediately on the girl, standing quietly, a little apart, looking up at the house. His first reaction was that she was not his type—or Paolo's, for that matter, and he found this faintly bewildering. In fact she fitted none of the preconceived images his aunt's fulminations had engendered, he thought critically as he observed her. Nearly as tall as Paolo himself, with clear, pale skin, a cloud of russet hair reaching to her shoulders, eyes like smoke, and a sweet, blunt-cornered mouth.

Not a conventional beauty—but curiously beguiling all the same.

Probably too slim, he mused, although the cheap dress she was wearing was singularly unrevealing.

And then, as if in answer to some silent wish, a faint breeze from the hills behind them blew the thin material back against her body, moulding it against the small, high breasts, the slight concavity of her stomach, the faintly rounded thighs, and long, slender legs.

Alessio, astonished, felt the breath catch suddenly in his throat, and, in spite of himself, he found his body stirring with frank and unexpected anticipation.

I've changed my mind, he thought in instant self-mockery. I

shan't get drunk after all. On the contrary, I think this *ragazza* deserves nothing less than my complete and sober attention.

He became aware that the Signora was approaching, her eyes studying him with disfavour.

'Is this how you dress to receive your visitors, Alessio?'

He took her hand, bowing over it. His smile glinted coldly at her. 'Ten minutes ago, Zia Lucrezia, I was not dressed at all. This is a concession.' He eyed Caio grimly. 'And you have brought your dog, I see. I hope he has learned better manners since our last encounter.' He looked past her to his cousin. 'Ah, Paolo, *come stai?*'

Paolo stared at him suspiciously. 'What are you doing here?'

Alessio gave him a look of mild surprise. 'It is my house, which makes me your host. Naturally, I wish to be here to attend to your comfort.'

'You are not usually so concerned,' Paolo muttered.

Alessio grinned at him. 'No? Then perhaps I have seen the error of my ways. And the house has enough rooms for us all. You will not be required to share with me, cousin,' he added blandly, then looked at the girl as if he had just noticed her. 'And the name of your charming companion?' Deliberately, he kept his voice polite rather than enthusiastic, noting the nervousness in the grey eyes under their dark fringe of lashes.

Paolo took her hand defensively. 'This is Signorina Laura Mason, who has come with me from London. Laura, may I present my cousin, the Count Alessio Ramontella.'

He saw that she did not meet his gaze, but looked down instead at the flagstoned courtyard. 'How do you do, *signore*?' Her voice was quiet and clear.

'Allow me to welcome you to my home, *signorina*.' He inclined his head with formal courtesy, then led the way into the house. 'Emilia, please show the ladies where they are to sleep. And the dog. Guillermo, will you take my cousin to his room?'

As he was turning away Paolo grabbed his arm. 'What is this?' he hissed. 'Where are you putting Laura?'

'In the room next to your mother's—at her request.' Alessio shrugged. 'I am sorry if you are disappointed, but you also know that she would never permit you to sleep with your girlfriend under any roof that she was sharing. Besides, if you even approach that part of the house, that little hairy rat of your *mamma's* will hear and start yapping.' His grin was laced with faint malice. 'Like the old monks, you will have to practise chastity.'

'A lesson you have yet to learn,' Paolo returned sourly.

'In general, perhaps, but I have never brought a woman here,' Alessio told him softly.

'Talking of which,' Paolo said, 'what do you think of my little English *inamorata*?'

'Do you need my opinion?' Alessio gave him a steady look. 'If she satisfies you, cousin, that should be enough.' He paused. 'Although usually you like them with more...' He demonstrated with his hands.

'*Sì,*' Paolo agreed lasciviously. 'But this girl has—hidden depths, if you take my meaning.' And he laughed.

It occurred to Alessio that he had never particularly liked his cousin, and at this moment it would give him great pleasure to smack him in the mouth.

Instead he invited him to make himself at home, and went off to his own room to shower and change.

Laura felt dazed as she followed Emilia and the Signora along a series of passages. The Villa Diana was a single-storey building, and it seemed to ramble on forever in a leisurely way. But she was in no mood to take real stock of her surroundings. Not yet.

That, she thought with disbelief, *that* was the Count Ramontella, the august head of the Arleschi Bank? That half-naked individual with the unruly mane of curling black hair, and the five o'clock shadow?

She'd assumed, when she first saw him, that he must be the caretaker, or the gardener.

She'd expected an older, staider version of Paolo, conventionally good-looking with a figure that would incline to plumpness in middle age. But the Count was fully six feet tall, with a lean, muscular golden-skinned body that she'd had every opportunity to admire. The shorts he'd been wearing, slung low on his narrow hips, just erred on the right side of decency, she thought, her face warming slightly at the recollection.

And he was nowhere near middle life—hardly more than in his early thirties, if she was any judge. Not, she supposed, that she was.

As for the rest of him—well, his face was more striking than handsome, with a high-bridged beak of a nose, a frankly cynical mouth, and eyes as dark as midnight that looked at the world with bored indifference from under their heavy lids. Or at least, she amended, that was the way he'd looked at her.

And he wasn't his aunt's greatest admirer either, as Paolo had suggested. She hadn't understood their brief exchange, but she'd detected a certain amount of snip, all the same.

But, if that was how he felt about his visitors, why was he here, when he wasn't expected and it was clear that he had better places to go? It seemed to make no sense.

Whatever, she could not imagine him being pleased to find he was entertaining a very minor cog from his London branch's PR machine. All the more reason, she told herself, for her connection with Harman Grace to remain a closely guarded secret. So— she'd continue to be the girl Paolo had met in a bar, and let his noble relative pick the bones out of that.

But her troubled musings ceased when Emilia, a comfortably built woman with a beaming smile, flung open a door with a triumphant, *'Ecco, signorina,'* indicating that this was her bed-room.

Laura took a step inside, and looked round, her eyes widening with delight. It couldn't have presented a greater contrast to the opulent and cluttered apartment where she'd stayed yesterday. For one thing, it was double the size of the room she'd occupied there, she realised, with a floor tiled in a soft pink marble, while the white plaster walls still bore traces of ancient frescos, which she would examine at her leisure.

But that was the only suggestion of the villa's age. For the present day, there was a queen-sized bed, prettily hung with filmy white curtains, which also graced the shuttered windows. A chest of drawers, a clothes cupboard, and a night table comprised the rest of the furniture, and a door led to a compact but luxurious shower room, tiled in the same shade of pink. The only other additions to the bedroom were a lamp beside the bed, and a bowl of roses on the chest.

She turned to Emilia. 'Perfect,' she said, smiling. And, managing to ignore Signora Vicente's disdainful glance, *'Perfetto.'*

When she was alone, she went over to the window, and pulled it wide. It opened, she saw, onto a three-sided courtyard, bordered by a narrow colonnade, like a medieval cloister, and she stepped through, gazing around her. There was a small fountain in the centre of the paved area, with a battered cherub pouring water from a shell into a shallow pool, while beside it stood a stone bench.

Directly ahead of her, Laura saw, the courtyard itself opened out into the sunlit grass and flowers of the garden beyond, and from somewhere not too far away she could hear the cooing of doves.

But it wasn't all peace and tranquillity, she realised wryly. From even closer at hand, she could hear the raised autocratic tones of the Signora, mingled with Emilia's quieter replies.

A salutary reminder that this little piece of Eden also had its serpents, not to mention wolves and bears, she thought, gazing up at the thickly forested slopes that brooded above her.

Suddenly, she felt tired, sticky and a little dispirited. She'd seen that there were towels and a range of toiletries waiting in the shower room, so decided she might as well make use of them.

She stood under the powerful jet of warm water, lathering her skin luxuriously with soap that smelt of lilies, feeling as if her anxieties were draining away with the suds and she were being somehow reborn, refreshed and invigorated.

Most of the towels were linen, but there were a couple of fluffy bath sheets as well, and when she was dry she wound herself in one of them, and trailed back into the bedroom.

While she'd been occupied, her case had arrived and was waiting on the bed, so she busied herself with unpacking. She hadn't brought nearly enough, she thought, viewing the results with dis-

favour, and very little that was smart or formal enough for someone who found herself staying with a count at his private villa.

The outfit that had survived with the fewest creases was a
wrap-around dress in a silver-grey silky material, and she decided
to try and create a good impression by wearing it for dinner that
night.

She had a solitary credit card, kept for emergencies, and maybe
she could persuade Paolo to risk the road from hell on a trip to
Perugia, so that she could supplement her wardrobe a little.

Whatever she wore, the Signora would sneer, and she accepted
that. But for reasons she could not explain, or even admit to, she
did not want Count Ramontella looking at her with equal disdain.

She wanted him to accept the fiction that she and Paolo were
an item. Perhaps to acknowledge, in some way she hadn't worked
out yet, that she was an eligible bride for his cousin, and welcome
her as such.

And pigs might fly, she thought morosely.

In the meantime, she wasn't sure what to do next. The whole
villa seemed enveloped in sleepy heat. There was even silence
from the adjoining room, the only sound being the faint soothing
splash of the fountain.

Laura felt she could hardly blunder about exploring her new
surroundings, alone and uninvited, in case she committed some
kind of social *faux pas*.

So, she decided, she was probably better off remaining where
she was until summoned.

She was just about to stretch out on the bed with her book
when there was a knock at the door.

Paolo, she thought instantly, wishing she were wearing something more reliable than a big towel. But when she cautiously
opened the door, and peeped round it, she found Emilia waiting
with a tray.

Beaming, the older woman informed her in halting English
that His Excellency thought the *signorina* might need some re-
freshment after her journey, then placed the tray in her hands
and departed.

Laura carried the tray over to the bed and set it down with

care. It held a teapot, with a dish of lemon slices, a plate of tiny crustless sandwiches containing some kind of pâté, and a bowl of golden cherries faintly flushed with crimson.

It was a kindness she had not anticipated, she thought with faint bewilderment. In fact the Count Ramontella seemed positively full of surprises.

But perhaps she was reading too much into this. Clearly his hospitality was primarily aimed at his aunt, and she'd been included as an afterthought.

Because her host didn't seem like a man who went in for random acts of kindness, Laura thought, remembering uneasily the faint curl of that beautifully moulded mouth.

So, she might as well make the most of this one, while it was on offer.

She ate every scrap of the delicious sandwiches with two cups of tea, then lay back with a contented sigh, savouring the cherries as she read. Later, she dozed for a while.

When she eventually awoke, the sun was much lower in the sky, and shadows were beginning to creep across the courtyard outside.

She donned a lacy bra and briefs, then sat down to make up her face with rather more care than usual, before giving her glossy fall of russet hair a vigorous brushing and fastening silver hoops in her ears. Finally, she sprayed her skin with the fresh, light scent she used, then slipped into the chosen dress, winding its sash round her slender waist and fastening it in a bow.

She'd brought one pair of flattish evening sandals in a neutral pewter shade—light years away from the glamorous shoes with their dizzyingly high heels that Italy was famous for. But even if she'd possessed such a pair, she wouldn't have been able to wear them, she conceded regretfully, because that would have made her slightly taller than Paolo, who was sensitive about his height.

Count Ramontella, of course, had no such concerns, she thought. The highest heels in the world would only have raised her to a level with his chin. And God only knew why such a thing had even occurred to her.

It was time she concentrated on Paolo, and the task she'd agreed to perform.

She let herself out of her bedroom, and started down the passage, trying to retrace her earlier steps. She had more time to observe her surroundings now, and she realised that the whole place was a series of courtyards, some completely enclosed, each of them marked by its own fountain, or piece of statuary.

And a good job too, because it's like a labyrinth, she thought, hesitating, totally at a loss, as the passage she was negotiating crossed another. To her relief, the white-coated manservant who had been at the entrance when they'd arrived appeared from nowhere, and indicated politely that she should follow him.

The room she was shown to was enormous, its focal point a huge stone fireplace surmounted by a coat of arms. It was also empty, and Laura hesitated in the doorway, feeling dwarfed by her surroundings, and a little isolated too.

Obviously, she had left her room much too early. The Italians, she recalled, were apt to dine later than people did in England, but she decided to stay where she was rather than attempt that maze of passages again.

She saw with interest that, in here, some restoration work had been done to the frescoed walls, and wandered round, taking a closer, fascinated look and speculating on their age. There were various hunting scenes, and, more peacefully, an outdoor feast with music and dancing, and the style of dress suggested the sixteenth century.

At the far end of the room, large floor-length windows stood open, leading out to a terrace from which a flight of steps descended, leading down to further gardens below.

Once again, furniture in the *salotto* had been kept to a minimum—a few massive sofas, their dimensions reduced by the proportions of the room, and a long, heavily carved sideboard were the main features. Also, more unusually, a grand piano.

It was open and, intrigued, Laura crossed to it and sat down on the stool, running her fingers gently over the keys, listening to its lovely, mellow sound.

She gave a small sigh. So many sad things had followed her

father's death, and the loss of her own much-loved piano was only one of them.

She tried a quiet chord or two, then, emboldened by the fact that she was still alone, launched herself into a modern lullaby that she had once studied as an exam piece.

Perhaps because it had always been a favourite of hers, she got through it without too much faltering, and sighed again as she played the final plangent notes, lost in her own nostalgic world.

She started violently as the music died to be replaced with the sound of someone clapping. She turned swiftly and apprehensively towards the doorway.

'*Bravo,*' said the Count Ramontella, and walked slowly across the room towards her.

CHAPTER FOUR

'OH CHRISTMAS,' Laura muttered under her breath, aware that she was blushing. 'I'm so sorry, *signore*. I didn't realise...' She swallowed. 'I had no right—no right at all...'

'*Nonsenso*. That was charming.' He came to lean against the corner of the piano, the dark eyes watching her coolly. He was totally transformed, she thought, having shaved, and combed his hair neatly back from his face. And he was wearing slim-fitting black trousers, which emphasised his long legs, offset by a snowy shirt, open at the throat, and topped by a crimson brocaded waistcoat, which he had chosen to leave unbuttoned.

He looked, Laura thought, swallowing again, casually magnificent.

'At last my decision to keep it in tune is justified,' he went on. 'It has not been played, I believe, since my mother died.'

'Oh, God, that makes everything worse.' She shook her head wretchedly. 'I must apologise again. This was—is—such an unforgivable intrusion.'

'But I do not agree,' he said. 'I think it delightful. Won't you play something else?'

'Oh, no.' She got up hastily, her embarrassment increasing, and was halted, the hem of her dress snagged on the protruding corner of the piano stool. 'Damn,' she added, jerking at the fabric, trying to release herself.

'*Sta' quieto,*' the Count commanded. 'Keep still, or you will tear it.' He dropped gracefully to one knee beside her, and deftly set her free.

She looked down at the floor. 'Thank you.'

'It is nothing.' He rose to his feet, glancing around him. 'What have you done with Paolo?'

'I—I haven't seen him since we arrived.'

46

'*Davvero?*' His brows lifted. 'I hope he is not neglecting you.' He sent her a faint smile. 'If so, you may be glad of the piano to provide you with entertainment.'

'Oh, no,' she said quickly. 'He isn't neglectful. Not at all.' She paused. 'Perhaps his mother wanted to talk to him.'

'If so, I think her revolting little dog would have told us all.' He was silent for a moment. 'Tell me, did you enjoy your afternoon tea?'

Her eyes flew to his dark face. 'You—really arranged that? That was very kind.'

He shrugged. 'We tend to have the evening meal later than you are used to in England. I did not wish you to faint with hunger.' He smiled at her pleasantly. 'You will soon become accustomed to Italian time.'

'I'll certainly try,' she said. 'But you can't make many adjustments in two weeks.'

His smile widened slightly. 'On the contrary, I think a great deal can change very quickly.' He walked over to the sideboard. 'May I get you a drink? I intend to have a whisky.'

'I'm fine—really.' She wasn't. Her throat felt as dry as a bone, and had done ever since she'd seen him standing there.

'There is orange juice,' he went on as if she hadn't spoken. 'Have you tried it with campari?'

'Well—no.'

'Then do so now.' He mixed the drink, and brought it to her. Touched his glass to hers. '*Salute.*'

'*Grazie,*' Laura said rather stiffly.

'*Prego.*' This time his smile was a grin. 'Tell me, *signorina*, are you always this tense?'

She sipped her drink, liking the way the sweetness of the juice blended with the bitterness of the campari. She said, haltingly, 'Not always, but this is a difficult situation for me.' She took a breath. 'You must be wondering, *signore*, what I'm doing here.'

'You came with my cousin,' he said. 'It is no secret.'

She took a deep breath. 'So, you must also know that his mother is not pleased about my presence.'

He drank some whisky, his eyes hooded. 'I do not concern

myself in my aunt's affairs, *signorina*.' He paused, and she saw that slight curl of the mouth again. 'At least, not unless they are forced upon my notice.'

She said rather forlornly, 'Just as I have been—haven't I?'

'Perhaps,' he said. 'But, believe me, *signorina*, now that we have met, I expect nothing but pleasure from your visit.' Before she could prevent him, he took her hand and raised it to his lips, kissing it lightly and swiftly.

The dark gaze glinted at her as he released her. 'Would it help you relax if we were a little less formal with each other? My name is Alessio, and I know that yours is Laura.'

She was aware that the colour had stormed back into her face. She said a little breathlessly, 'I think your aunt might object.'

His tone was silky. 'Then let us agree to leave her to her own devices, *si*?'

'Yes,' she said. 'If you're quite sure.'

'I am certain.' He paused. 'Shall we take our drinks onto the terrace? It is pleasant there in the evenings.'

Laura followed reluctantly. She hadn't bargained for this, she thought uneasily. She'd expected Paolo to be hovering constantly, acting as a barrier between her and his family.

There was a table on the terrace, and comfortable cushioned chairs. Alessio held one for her courteously, then took the adjoining seat. There was a silence, and Laura took a nervous sip of her drink.

'You and Paolo aren't very alike—for cousins,' she ventured at last.

'No,' Alessio said, contemplating his whisky. 'There is very little resemblance between us. Physically, I believe he favours his late father.'

'I see.' She hesitated, then said in a small wooden voice, 'His mother, the Signora, is a very—striking woman.'

'She has a forceful personality, certainly,' he said drily. 'I understand that, when she was young, she was also considered a great beauty.' He leaned back in his chair. 'Tell me, Laura, how did you meet my cousin?'

'I work in a wine bar,' she said. 'He was one of the customers.'

'Ah,' he said. 'So you are not always as shy as you are with me.'

'But then,' she returned, 'I wasn't expecting to meet you, *signore*.'

'You have forgotten,' he said. 'We agreed it would be Alessio.'

No, she thought. I haven't forgotten a thing. I'm not ready to be on first-name terms—or any terms at all—with someone like you.

There was a loud sneeze from inside the *salotto*, and Paolo emerged, flourishing a large handkerchief. '*Maledizione*, I am getting a cold,' he said peevishly. 'Some germ on the plane, *indubbiamente*.'

Laura decided this was her cue. 'Darling.' She got up and went to his side, sliding her arm through his. 'How horrid for you. Summer colds are always the worst.'

For a second, he looked at her as if he'd forgotten who she was, then he pulled himself together, kissing her rather awkwardly on the cheek. 'Well, I must take care not to pass it on to you, *carissima. Che peccato*, eh? What a pity.' He slid an arm round her, his fingers deliberately brushing the underside of her breast.

Laura, nailing on a smile, longed to pull away and kick him where it hurt. Alessio drank some more whisky, his face expressionless.

If she'd hoped that the arrival of his mother a short while later would impose some constraint upon Paolo, Laura was doomed to disappointment. He'd drawn his chair close beside hers at the table, and appeared glued to her side, his hand stroking her arm and shoulder possessively, his lips never far from her ear, her hair, or her cheek, nibbling little caresses that she found positively repellent.

She knew, of course, that the Signora was watching, her mouth drawn into a tight line, because that was the purpose of the exercise. And there was nothing she could do about it. But she was also sharply aware that the Count was sending them the odd meditative glance, and this, for some reason, she found even more disturbing than the older woman's furious scrutiny.

She found she was silently repeating, 'Think of the money. Think of the money,' over and over again like a mantra, but it was not producing the desired calming effect, and she was thankful to her heart when dinner was finally announced, and Paolo reluctantly had to relinquish his hold.

The dining room was a long, low-ceilinged room, with a wonderful painted ceiling depicting some Bacchanalian revel, with people wearing bunches of grapes instead of clothes.

The scene below was much more decorous, the polished table gleaming with silver and crystal in the light of several elaborate candelabra. Alessio sat at the head of the table, with his aunt facing him at its foot, and Laura was seated halfway down, opposite Paolo, the width of the table putting her beyond the reach of any more amorous overtures.

Not that he seemed in the mood any longer. Instead he kept sighing, blowing his nose, and occasionally putting a hand to his forehead, as if checking his own temperature.

In spite of her concerns, Laura found she was really hungry, and tucked into the wild mushroom risotto, the veal in a rich wine sauce, and the creamy almond-flavoured dessert that she was offered with a good appetite. But she was far more sparing with the wine that Guillermo tried to pour into her glass, recognising that she needed to keep her wits about her.

Conversation was kept to general topics, and conducted in English. The Signora tried a few times to switch to Italian, but was forestalled by the Count, who silkily reminded her that she was overlooking the presence of their guest, so that she was forced to subside, glaring.

The meal was almost over when Paolo dropped his bombshell. '*Mamma*—the ring that my grandmother left me, which you keep in the safe at the *appartamento*. You will give it to me when we return to Rome, if you please?'

The ensuing silence was electric. Laura kept her eyes fixed on her plate. Oh, God, she wailed inwardly. What possessed him to say that—and why didn't he warn me?

Whatever she herself might think of the Signora, and no matter what disagreement over the future Paolo might be engaged in with her, the older woman was still his mother—and he was deliberately taunting her. Pushing his supposed relationship to new limits.

She thought, biting her lip, This is so wrong...

'It is a valuable piece of jewellery,' the Signora said at last, her voice shaking a little. 'It needs to be kept in security. But of course, *figlio mio*, it is for you to decide.'

'And I have done so.' Paolo sent her a bland smile. 'It is time it was in my keeping.'

Laura put down her spoon, unable to eat another mouthful. Across the candle flames, she sent Paolo a condemnatory look.

After that the conversation flagged, and she was thankful when the Count suggested that they have coffee in the *salotto*.

It was served black and very strong in small cups.

'*Grappa* for the *signorina*.' Guillermo proffered a tiny glass of colourless liquid, and she glanced across at Paolo, whose expression was so smug she could have slapped him.

'What is *grappa*?' she asked.

'A kind of brandy,' he said. 'Good for the digestion.'

For medicinal purposes only, Laura thought, raising the glass to her lips. She took one cautious sip, and nearly choked, eyes streaming.

'My God,' she said when she could speak, accepting the glass of mineral water that Alessio handed her. 'How strong is that?'

'About ninety-per-cent proof,' he told her, amused. 'You have never drunk it before?'

'No,' she said with feeling. 'I would definitely have remembered.'

The Count looked at his cousin. 'Paolo, you have neglected Laura's education.'

Paolo stopped mopping his face long enough to leer. '*Al contrario*, my dear Alessio, I've been concentrating on the things that matter.'

Alessio gave him a thoughtful look, but made no comment, while Laura sat, her face burning, wishing the floor would open.

The Signora, who had been sitting like a stone statue in a corner of the sofa, abruptly announced her intention of watching television, which, Laura discovered, was housed in a large carved cabinet in the corner of the room. It was some kind of current affairs programme, which she was unable to follow, so her interest soon waned.

Instead, she watched the chess game now in progress between the two men. She was no expert, but it was soon obvious that Paolo had got himself into an impossible position.

'I feel too ill to play,' he said peevishly as he resigned. 'I shall tell Emilia to make a *tisana* and bring it to my bedroom.'

He pushed back his chair and got up, kissing Laura on the cheek. 'Goodnight, *carissima*. If I sleep now, I shall be well tomorrow, so that we can spend some time alone together, and I can show you my beautiful country. Starting maybe with Assisi, hmm?'

Laura forced a smile, and murmured that it would be wonderful.

He kissed his mother's hand, ignored the basilisk glance she sent him, and disappeared.

Alessio moved the pieces back to the starting point and looked up at Laura. 'Would you like to challenge the winner?' he asked.

'After the way you dealt with Paolo, I don't think so.' Her tone was rueful. 'You need my young brother. He was school chess champion when he was six.'

'Your brother?' the Signora suddenly interrupted. 'I thought you were an only child, *signorina*.'

Laura realised too late that was what she'd agreed with Paolo. Not just an only child, but an orphan too. It would save them many problems if she was without family, he'd decreed. And she'd just blown it.

Which meant she would have to warn him first thing tomorrow about her unguarded words.

In the meantime: 'Is that the impression I gave, *signora*?' She made herself speak lightly. 'It was probably wishful thinking.' She paused. 'And now, perhaps you'll excuse me, too. It's been a long day, and I still have to negotiate the maze back to my room.'

Alessio rose. 'Permit me,' he said. He walked to the fireplace and tugged at the bell-pull that hung there. A moment later, Guillermo appeared, his face enquiring. 'The *signorina* is ready to retire. Please escort her,' he directed quietly.

Laura was still suddenly, aware of an odd disappointment. Then: 'Thank you,' she said stiltedly. 'And—goodnight.'

Alessio watched in silence as she followed Guillermo from the room.

As soon as they had gone the Signora was on her feet with a hiss of impatience. 'Are you mad? Why did you not take her to her room yourself? It was your chance to be alone with the little fool.'

His mouth tightened in the knowledge he had been sorely tempted to do exactly that, and had deliberately resisted the impulse. 'I know what I am doing,' he told her curtly. 'Or do you want her to take fright, and scuttle off to Paolo for sanctuary?'

'Take fright?' she echoed contemptuously. 'That one? What are you talking about?'

Alessio sighed. 'I merely wish to point out that she does not seem a girl one would pick up in a bar. I am—surprised.'

She gave a harsh laugh. 'So that look of mock innocence has deceived you, my worldly nephew, as it has my poor boy.' She spread her hand. 'Can you doubt how besotted he is with her? To ask for Nonna Caterina's ring so brazenly. The ring I planned for him to give to Beatrice. I could not believe it.'

'Neither, I think, could she,' Alessio said drily. 'Are you really so sure they are in love, or does he simply wish to sell the ring to pay off his gambling debts?'

'Love?' She almost spat the word, ignoring his jibe. 'What does that mean? She is attracted by my son's background—his position in the world. She believes he is also wealthy.'

'Then show her his bank statements,' Alessio said coldly. 'That will cure her, and save me a great deal of trouble.'

'But it will not cure him. You saw him this evening. He could not keep his hands off her.'

'So it would seem,' Alessio agreed slowly. 'It is as well, perhaps, that they are sleeping at opposite ends of the house.'

'You have forgotten this sightseeing tour tomorrow.' The Signora frowned. 'No doubt they will go only as far as the nearest hotel willing to rent them a room for a few hours.'

Alessio felt his mouth twist with sudden and profound distaste at the image her words conjured up, and denounced himself with silent savagery for being a hypocrite.

He said icily, 'Then I suggest, my dear aunt, that you too develop a sudden interest in the local attractions. You have not, after all, seen the Giotto frescos in the basilica at Assisi since their restoration. Go with them, and act as chaperon, if you think it is necessary. And take the dog with you. Teach him to bite Paolo each time he touches the girl.'

'Oh, there is no reasoning with you when you are in this mood.' The Signora swept to the door. 'I will bid you goodnight.' She turned and gave him a measuring look. 'But our agreement still stands. Be in no doubt of that.'

When he was alone, Alessio walked over to the piano, and stood picking out a few notes with one finger, his face thoughtful. He found himself remembering the delicate flush that had warmed Laura's pale skin when she'd looked up and seen him watching and listening in the doorway. Recalled even more acutely how her clean fragrance had assailed his senses as he'd knelt beside her to free her skirt.

The dress had been a beguiling one altogether, he thought. In other circumstances it would have been so simple to release the sash, and let it fall apart, revealing the warm sweetness beneath the silvery folds. So enticing to touch her as he wished, and feel her smooth skin under his mouth.

He found himself smiling, wondering if she would blush as deeply when she was aroused.

Not a wise thought to take to bed with you, he told himself wryly as he began to turn off the lights in the room. And he must be insane to indulge in this kind of adolescent fantasy about a girl he needed to keep, coolly and clinically, on the far edge of his life. But, then, only a fool would have allowed himself to be caught in this kind of trap in the first place.

And found he was sighing with unexpected bitterness as he walked to the door.

It was a long time before Laura fell asleep that night. She was tired, but aware of too many disturbing vibrations in the house to be able to relax completely. And her one recurring thought was that she was no longer sure she could go on with this charade, which was becoming far too complicated.

And, she suspected, unmanageable.

What was Paolo going to demand she did next? she asked herself, exasperated. Actually become engaged to him?

Once she'd got him to herself tomorrow, she would be able to talk to him seriously, she thought with determination. Persuade him that things had gone far enough, and his mother had been given sufficient shocks to last a lifetime. Surely the Signora must be convinced by now that her plan to marry him off was dead in the water—especially after that stunt he'd pulled at dinner, she thought grimly. They didn't need to take any more risks.

Now, somehow, she had to persuade him to take her away from the Villa Diana. Or, if she was really honest, separate her from its owner.

In spite of the heat, she found herself shivering.

She had been following Guillermo through the passages when it had suddenly hit her just how much she'd been hoping that the Count himself would offer to accompany her.

And how many kinds of madness was that? she asked herself with a kind of despair.

She'd been in his company for only a few hours, and already her awareness of him was threatening to spin out of control.

For God's sake, grow up, she told herself wearily, giving the pillows a thump.

Yes, there'd been times when the courtesy she knew he'd have shown to any guest under his roof had seemed to slip into kindness, but that could have been an attempt to make amends for his aunt's unfailing rudeness. And she'd be fooling herself if she thought otherwise, even for a moment.

The Arleschi Bank was considered a model of its kind, keenly efficient, highly respected, and superbly profitable, which was why Harman Grace were so keen to represent it. And it was clear that the bank's chairman played a key role in its achievements.

Count Alessio Ramontella lived in the full radiance of the sun, Laura thought, whereas she occupied some small, cold planet on the outmost edge of the solar system. That was the way it was, and always would be. And it was her bad luck that their paths had ever been forced to cross.

She closed her eyes against the memory of his smile, its sudden brilliance turning the rather ruthless lines of his mouth to charm and humour. She tried to forget, too, the warmth of that swift brush of his lips on her hand, and the way even that most fleeting of touches had pierced her to the bone.

It occurred to her that if Steve's kisses had carried even a fraction of the same shattering charge, he'd probably have been a happy man at this very moment, and Paolo would have had to look elsewhere for a partner in his scam.

I really need to get away from here, she told herself, moving restlessly, feeling the fine linen sheet that covered her grazing her skin as if it were raw. And soon.

It could be managed, of course, and quite easily. Paolo could pretend to take her on the visit to Tuscany they'd originally planned. Once they were alone, who would ever know if she slipped away and took an early flight back to London? And as long as Paolo kept a low profile, he could spend his vacation time exactly as he wished.

It wasn't what she wanted—it saddened her that she wouldn't see Florence or any of the region's other proud cities—but it was clear that she could no longer trust Paolo. And it was a way of dealing with a problem that was threatening to snowball into a crisis, entirely through her own stupidity.

Not that she could ever tell Paolo that. This was another truth that would have to be suppressed.

And he never wanted to come here in the first place, she thought. So he can hardly complain if I say I want to leave.

She turned over, burying her face determinedly in the pillow. And if her sleep was haunted by dreams, they did not linger to be remembered in the morning.

The determination, however, persisted, stronger than ever, and Laura sang softly to herself as she showered and dressed in a blue denim skirt and a sleeveless white top.

It was another glorious day, with the sun already burning off the faint haze around the tops of the hills. Probably her last day in Italy, she thought, and she would make the most of every minute.

She and Paolo would sort everything on the trip to Assisi, and by tomorrow they could be out of here, and life could return to normal again.

She would even learn to laugh about the last couple of days. Make a good story out of the Signora. Tell Gaynor, 'Hey, I met a man who was the ultimate sex on a stick, and fabulously wealthy too.' Let it all sound like fun, without a moment of self-doubt, she thought as she brushed her hair.

She had taken careful note of the route to the main part of the house the previous night, and found the dining room without difficulty, only to discover that it was deserted with no sign of food.

They eat dinner late, maybe breakfast is the same, she thought, slightly nonplussed. As she was wandering back into the entrance hall she was swooped on by Emilia, who led her firmly into the *salotto* and indicated that she should go out onto the terrace.

She emerged cautiously and paused in dismay, because Alessio was there alone, seated at the table, which was now covered by a white cloth. A few feet away, in the shade, a large trolley was stationed, and she saw that it held a platter with ham on the bone, together with a dish of cheese, a basket of bread rolls and a bowl of fruit. A pot of coffee was keeping warm on a heater.

'*Buon giorno.*' He had seen her, and, putting down the news-

paper he was reading, rose to his feet, depriving her of the chance
to retreat back into the villa. 'You rested well?'

'Yes—thank you.' Reluctantly, she took the seat he indicated
and unfolded her napkin, glancing at the table. 'Only two
places?' Her brow furrowed. 'Where are the others?'

'They are breakfasting in their rooms,' Alessio told her. 'My
aunt, because she prefers it. Paolo, because he is too ill to leave
his bed,' he added sardonically.

'Too ill?' Laura echoed, taking the glass of chilled peach juice
he'd poured for her. 'What do you mean?'

He shrugged. 'His cold. It has become infinitely worse. His
mother is most concerned. Every lemon we possess is being
squeezed to make drinks for him, and she has commandeered
every painkiller in the house.'

'Oh.' Laura digested this, her dismay deepening by the second.
She had not bargained for this development. She said, 'Perhaps
I'd better go to him, too. See how he is, and if I can help.'

'A word of advice, *bella mia*,' Alessio said lazily. 'A wolf, a
bear and my aunt Lucrezia—never come between any of them
and their cubs. So, stay where you are, and eat. You will be
much safer, I promise you.'

He got to his feet, lithe in cream denim trousers and a black
polo shirt, and went to the trolley. 'May I bring you some of this
excellent ham?'

'Thank you.' She watched him carve several slices off the
bone with deft precision. As he placed the plate in front of her
she said, 'Maybe he'll feel better later on, and be able to get up.
We're supposed to be going to Assisi.'

'Paolo will be going nowhere for the foreseeable future,'
Alessio said calmly. 'Unless his mother insists on my summoning
a helicopter to take him to the nearest hospital, of course.'

'He has a cold in the head.' Laura's mouth tightened. 'It's
hardly terminal.'

'It would be inadvisable to say so in front of Zia Lucrezia.'
Alessio ate a forkful of ham. 'Not that we will see much of her
either,' he added meditatively. 'Her time will be taken up with
nursing the invalid, smoothing his pillow, reading aloud to him,

and bullying my poor Emilia into creating little delicacies to tempt his failing appetite.'

Laura finished her peach juice, and set down the glass. She said slowly, 'You're really serious about this.'

'No, but my aunt is. However,' he added silkily, 'I gather that, with rest and quiet, the prognosis is generally favourable.'

In spite of her private concerns, Laura found herself laughing. 'It's just so absurd. All this fuss about a cold.'

'Ah, but it is the areas of fuss that matter in marriage, I am told,' Alessio said blandly. 'It is best to discover what they are before the ceremony, and you have now been given a valuable insight into Paolo's concerns about his health.'

He watched with interest as Laura began to cut her ham into small, careful squares.

'You plan to marry my cousin, of course?' he added after a pause.

Her eyes flew warily to his face. 'I—I think...I mean—there's nothing formal. Not yet.'

'But you are travelling with him in order to meet his family. And last night it seemed certain,' he said. 'For the Vicentes, as for the Ramontellas, the giving of a ring—particularly an heirloom—is a serious thing. A declaration of irrevocable intent. One man, one woman bound in love for the rest of their lives.'

'Oh.' She swallowed. 'I didn't know that. He—didn't tell me.'

'And now you must wait until he recovers from this trying cold,' Alessio agreed, adding briskly, 'Would you like coffee, or shall I tell Emilia to bring you tea?'

Her mind had gone into overdrive, and she had to drag herself back to the present moment. 'Oh—coffee would be fine.'

She took the cup he brought her with a murmur of thanks.

'You seem a little upset,' he commented as he resumed his seat. 'May I know the problem?'

'It's nothing, really.' She bit her lip. 'Just that I feel a bit useless and in the way with Paolo being ill.' She tried to smile. 'I shan't know what to do with myself.'

'Then I suggest you relax.' He pointed to the steps. 'They lead down to the swimming pool, a pleasant place to sunbathe—and dream about the future, perhaps.'

He smiled at her. 'And try not to worry too much about Paolo,' he advised lightly. 'He has about six colds a year. You will have plenty of opportunity to nurse him, I promise.'

She put down her cup, staring at him suspiciously. 'You're making fun of me.'

'Well, a little, perhaps.' The smile widened into a grin. 'Teasing you is almost irresistible, believe me.'

He pushed away his plate and sat back in his chair, regarding her. 'But allow me to make amends. I have to go out presently on a matter of business in the village. But if you came with me, we could combine it with pleasure by driving on to Assisi. There is much to see there, and a good restaurant where we can have lunch. Would you like that?'

There was a tingling silence. Laura's look of uncertainty deepened.

She said, 'You—you're offering to take me to Assisi.' To her discomfiture, she felt herself beginning to blush. 'That—that's very kind of you, *signore*, and I—I'm grateful. But I couldn't put you to all that trouble—not possibly.'

'But it would be no trouble,' he said. '*Al contrario*, I would find it delightful.' He paused deliberately. 'But I notice that you still have a problem calling me by my given name, so perhaps you feel you cannot yet trust me enough to spend a day alone with me.'

Or perhaps it is yourself you do not trust, *bella mia*, he added silently, watching the colour flare in her face. And if so—you are mine.

'N-no,' she stammered. 'Oh, no. It's not that—not that at all.' She cast around frantically for an excuse—any excuse. 'You see—it's Paolo. The Assisi trip was his idea, and maybe I should wait until he's better, and we can go together. I—I don't want to hurt his feelings. Can you understand that?'

'Of course,' he said. 'I understand perfectly, believe me.' More than you think or wish, my sweet one, he added under his breath.

He sighed with mock reproach. 'However, I am distressed that

my shattered hopes do not concern you. Now that is cruel. But
if I cannot persuade you, so be it.'

And when the time comes, he thought as he pushed back his
chair and rose to his feet, some day—some night soon—then I
will make you come to me. Because you are going to want me
so much that you will offer yourself, my shy, lovely girl. Make
no mistake about that. And I will take everything you have to
give, and more.

Aloud, he said, '*Arriverderci*, Laura.' His smile was pleasant—even slightly impersonal as he looked down at her. 'Enjoy
your solitude while you can,' he added softly.

And he walked away, humming gently under his breath, while
Laura stared after him, still floundering in her own confusion.

CHAPTER FIVE

LAURA finished applying sun lotion to her arms and legs, and lay back in the shade of the big striped umbrella with a little sigh of contentment. Contrary to her own expectations, she was enjoying her solitude. The pool area occupied an extended hollow at the foot of the gardens, offering a welcome haven of tranquillity, with its marble tiles surrounding a large rectangle of turquoise water, and overlooked by terraced banks of flowering shrubs.

It was sheltered and very private, and, apart from birdsong and the hum of insects, it was also wonderfully quiet.

She put on her sunglasses and applied herself to taking an intelligent interest in her book, but the heroine's ill-starred attempts to pursue entirely the wrong man struggled to hold her attention, and at last she put the thing down, sighing impatiently.

In view of her current circumstances, it wasn't the ideal plot to engage her, she thought ruefully. In fact, *War and Peace* might have been a more appropriate choice. Especially as she'd just been totally routed by the enemy.

She'd managed to waylay a harassed Emilia, asking politely if she'd find out when it would be convenient for her to visit Paolo. But the reply conveyed back from the Signora was unequivocal. Paolo had a high fever but was now sleeping, so could not be disturbed.

If I were genuinely in love with him, I'd be chewing my nails to the quick by now, Laura thought indignantly.

But it was clear she had to start practising patience, and hope that, when his temperature eventually went down, Paolo would demand to see her instead.

She sighed. God, what a situation to be in, and all her own stupid doing, too. Why hadn't she remembered there was no such thing as a free lunch?

But the deep indolent heat was already soothing her, encouraging her to close her eyes and relax. Reminding her that it was pointless to fret, because, for the time being at least, she was no longer in control of her own destiny.

Che sera, sera, she thought drowsily, removing her sunglasses and nestling further into the soft cushions of the lounger. Whatever will be, will be. Isn't that what they say? So I may as well go with the flow. Especially as I don't seem to have much of a choice.

She closed her eyes. Oh, Paolo. She sent the silent plea winging passionately to the villa. For heaven's sake get well quickly, and get me out of here.

Alessio parked the Jeep in front of the house, and swung himself out of the driving seat. He needed, he thought as he strode indoors, a long cold drink, and a swim.

What he did not require was the sudden appearance of his aunt, as if she'd been lying in wait for him.

'Where have you been?' she demanded, and he checked resignedly.

'Down to the village. Luca Donini asked me to talk to his father—persuade him not to spend another winter in that hut of his.'

'He asked you?' Her brows lifted haughtily. 'But how can this concern you? Sometimes, Alessio, I think you forget your position.'

He gave her a long, hard look. 'Yes, Zia Lucrezia,' he drawled. 'Sometimes, I do, as the events of the past few weeks have unhappily proved. But Besavoro is my village, and the concerns of my friends there are mine too.'

She snorted impatiently. 'You did not take the girl with you?'

He shrugged. 'I invited her, but she refused me.'

She glared at him. 'That is bad. You cannot be trying.'

'No,' he said. 'It is better than I expected after such a short time.' His smile was cold. 'But do not ask me to explain.'

She changed tack. 'You should have told me you were going

to the village. You could have gone to the pharmacy for my poor boy. Last night he was delirious—talking nonsense in his sleep.'

'It is probably a habit of his,' Alessio commented curtly. 'Why not ask his *innamorata*?'

She gave him a furious look, and swept back to her nursing duties.

Alessio proceeded moodily to his room. The jibe had been almost irresistible, but he regretted it. There'd been no need to remind himself that Laura and Paolo had been enjoying an intimate relationship prior to their arrival in Italy. Because he knew it only too well already.

But what he could not explain was why he found it so galling. After all, he thought, he had never felt jealous or possessive about any of his previous involvements. For him, sex was usually just another appetite to be enjoyably and mutually satisfied. And there was nothing to be gained by jealousy or speculation over other lovers.

He'd awaited Laura's arrival at the villa with a sense of blazing resentment, even though he knew he had only himself to blame for his predicament, and, instead, found himself instantly intrigued by her. From that, it had only been a brief step to desire. And he strongly suspected this would have happened if he'd met her somewhere far from his aunt's interference.

He remembered, with distaste, icily promising to send her home with a beautiful memory. Now he wasn't sure he'd send her back at all. Certainly not immediately, he thought, frowning as he stripped and found a pair of brief black swimming trunks.

Maybe he'd whisk her away somewhere—the Seychelles or the Maldives, perhaps, or the Bahamas—for a few weeks of exotic pampering, with a quick trip to Milan first, of course, to reinvent her wardrobe. Buy her the kind of clothes he would enjoy removing.

And on that enticing thought he collected a towel and his sunglasses, and went down to the pool to find her.

He found her peacefully asleep, the long lashes curling on her cheek, her head turned slightly to one side. The sun had moved round, leaving one ankle and foot out in the open, vulnerable to its direct rays, and he reached up to make a slight adjustment to the parasol.

Having done so, he did not move away immediately, but stood for a moment, looking down at her. In the simple dark green one-piece swimsuit, her slender body looked like the stem of a flower, her hair crowning it like an exotic corolla of russet petals.

A single strand lay across her cheek, and he was tempted to smooth it back, but knew he could not risk so intimate a gesture.

Because he wanted her so fiercely, so unequivocally, it was like a blow in the guts. However, now was not yet the moment, so he would have to practise unaccustomed restraint, he reminded himself grimly.

Swallowing, he turned away, tossing his towel and sunglasses onto an adjoining lounger, then walked to the edge of the pool and dived in, his body cutting the water as cleanly as a knife.

Dimly, Laura heard the splash and came awake, lifting herself onto one elbow as she looked around her, faintly disorientated.

Then her eyes went to the pool, and the tanned body sliding with powerful grace through the water, and her mind cleared, with an instantaneous nervous lurch of the stomach.

Stealthily, she watched him complete another two lengths of the pool, then turn towards the side. She retrieved her sunglasses and slid them on, then grabbed her book, holding it in front of her like a barrier as Alessio lifted himself lithely out of the water and walked towards her, his body gleaming, sleek as a seal, in the sunlight.

'*Ciao.*' His smile was casual as he began to blot the moisture from his skin with his towel.

'Hello,' she responded hesitantly, not looking at him directly. Those trunks, she thought, her mouth drying, were even briefer than his shorts had been. She hurried into speech. 'You—you're back early. Did you settle all your business?'

'Not as I wished.' He grimaced. 'I had a battle of wills with a stubborn old man and lost.'

'Well,' she said. 'That can't happen too often.'

'It does with Fredo.' His face relaxed into a grin. 'He cannot forget that his son and I grew up together, and that he was almost a second father to me when my parents were away. He even took his belt to Luca and myself with complete impartiality when we behaved badly, and likes to remind me of it when he can.'

He shrugged. 'But he also showed us every track and trail in the forest, and taught us to use them safely. He even took me on my first wild boar hunt.'

'So why are you disagreeing now? Not that it's any of my business,' she added hastily.

'It's no secret. Even when his wife was alive, he did not like life in town, so when she died he moved up to a hut on the mountain to look after his goats there. He has been there ever since, and Luca worries that he is getting too old for such a life. He wants his father to live with him, but Fredo says his daughter-in-law is a bad cook, and has a tongue as sharp as a viper's bite, and I could not argue with that.'

'Absolutely not,' she agreed solemnly. 'A double whammy, no less.'

He laughed. 'As you say, *bella mia*. But the campaign is not over yet.'

'You don't give up easily.'

'I do not give up at all.'

He spread his towel on the lounger and stretched out, nodding at the book she was still clutching. 'Is it good?'

'The jacket says it's a best-seller.'

'Ah,' he said, softly. 'But what does Laura say?'

'That the jury's still out, but the verdict will probably be guilty. Murder by cliché.' She sighed. 'However, it's all I brought with me, so I have to make it last.'

'There are English books in my library up at the villa,' he said. 'Some classics, and some modern. You are welcome to borrow them. Ask Emilia to show you where they are.'

'Thank you, that's—very kind.' Her brows lifted in surprise. 'Is that why your English is so incredibly good—because you read a lot?'

'I learned English as a second language at school,' he said. 'And attended university in Britain and America.' His grin teased her. 'And it is fortunate that I did, as your Italian is so minimal.'

'But my French isn't bad,' she defended herself. 'If I'd gone on the holiday I originally planned, I'd have shone.'

'Ah,' he said. 'And what holiday was that?'

She was suddenly still, cursing herself under her breath. She'd let her tongue run away with her again. 'I thought of the Riviera,' she said. 'But then I met Paolo—and changed my mind, of course.'

'Of course.' She thought she detected a note of irony in his voice.

'Perhaps you should have stuck to plan A,' he went on. 'Then you would have avoided a meeting with Zia Lucrezia.'

'Indeed,' she said lightly. 'And Paolo might not have caught a cold.'

'Not with you to keep him warm, I am sure,' he said softly, and watched with satisfaction as the inevitable blush rose in her face. 'Have you been to see him?'

'I tried,' she admitted. 'But his mother wouldn't allow it. Apparently he's running a temperature.'

'Which you might raise to lethal limits.' He paused. 'And she may have a point,' he added silkily. 'But would you like me to speak to her for you—persuade her to see reason?'

'Would you?' she asked doubtfully. 'But why?'

'Who am I to stand in the way of love?' He shrugged a negligent shoulder, and Laura tried to ignore the resultant ripple of muscle.

Abruptly, she said, 'Do you know Beatrice Manzone?'

'I have met her,' he said. 'Why do you ask?'

'I was wondering what she was like.'

The dark gaze narrowed. 'What does Paolo say?'

She bit her lip. 'That she's rich.'

'A little harsh,' he said. 'She is also pretty and docile.' He grinned faintly. 'And cloying, like an overdose of honey. Quite unlike you, *mia cara*.'

She bit her lip. 'I wasn't looking for comparisons.'

'Then what do you want? Reassurance?' There was a sudden crispness in his tone. 'You should look to Paolo for that. And according to him, the Manzone girl is history.'

'His mother doesn't seem to think so.'

There was an odd silence, then he said, '*Mia bella*, if you and Paolo want each other, then what else matters?' He swung himself off the lounger, as if suddenly impatient. 'And now it is time we went up to the house for some lunch.'

Once again only two places had been set for the meal, which, this time, was being served in the coolness of the dining room. And her seat, Laura observed uneasily, had been moved up the table to within touching distance of his. It made serving the food more convenient, but at the same time it seemed as if she was constantly being thrust into close proximity with him—suddenly an honoured guest rather than an unwanted visitor—and she found this disturbing for all kinds of reasons.

But in spite of her mental reservations, her morning in the fresh air had certainly sharpened her appetite, and she ate her way through a bowl of vegetable soup, and a substantial helping of pasta. But her eyes widened in genuine shock when Guillermo carried the next course—a dish of cod baked with potatoes and parmesan—to the table.

'More food?' She shook her head. 'I don't believe it.'

Alessio looked amused. 'And there is still cheese and dessert to follow. You are going to be an Italian's wife, Laura. You must learn to eat well in the middle of the day.'

'But how can anyone do any work after all this?'

'No one does.' Alessio handed her a plate of food. 'Has Paolo not introduced you to the charms of the siesta?' He kept his voice light with an effort, knowing fiercely that he wanted to be the one to share with her those quiet, shuttered afternoon hours. To sleep with her wrapped in his arms, then wake to make slow, lazy love.

'We rest and work later when it is cooler,' he added, refilling her glass with wine.

'I think Paolo is used to London hours now,' she said, looking down at her plate.

'But he will not always work there, you understand.' He gave her a meditative look. 'How would you like living in Turin—or Milan?'

'I haven't thought about it.'

'Or,' he said slowly, 'it might even be Rome.'

She said, 'Oh, I expect I'd adjust—somehow.'

Except, she thought, that it will never happen, and began to make herself eat.

She wished with sudden desperation that she could confide in him. Tell him exactly why she was here, and how Paolo had persuaded her into this charade.

But there was no guarantee that he would understand, and he might not appreciate being made a fool of, and having his hospitality abused in such a way.

And although he and his aunt were plainly not on the best of terms, he might disapprove of the older woman being deliberately deceived.

Besides, and more importantly, thought Laura, it would render her even more vulnerable where he was concerned, and she could not afford that.

She'd come this far, she told herself rather wanly. She might as well go on to the bitter end—whenever that might be.

His voice broke across her reverie. 'What are you thinking?'

Quickly she forced a smile. Spoke eagerly. 'Oh, just how good it will be to see Paolo again. We don't seem to have been alone together for ages.' She managed a note of anxiety. 'You really do think you'll be able to persuade your aunt?'

'Yes,' Alessio said quietly, after a pause. 'Yes, I do.'

And they ate the rest of the meal in silence.

Siestas were probably fine in theory, thought Laura. In practice, they didn't seem to work quite so well. Or not for her, anyway.

She lay staring up at the ceiling fan, listening to its soft swish as it rotated, and decided she had never felt so wide awake. She needed something to occupy her.

Her book was finished, its ending as predictable as the rest of the story, and she had no wish to lie about thinking. Because her mind only seemed to drift in one direction—towards the emotional minefield presided over by the Count Alessio Ramontella.

And it was ludicrous—pathetic—to allow herself to think about a man who, a week ago, had been only a name on the paperwork from the Arleschi Bank's head office. A distant figurehead, and nothing more.

And no matter how attractive he might be, that was how he would always remain—remote. No part of any world that she lived in, except for these few dreamlike, unforgettable days.

Except that she had to forget them—and pretty damned quickly too—as soon as she returned to England, if not before.

She slid off the bed. She'd have a shower, she decided, and wash her hair. She'd brought no dryer with her, but twenty minutes or so with a hairbrush in the courtyard's afternoon sun would serve the same purpose.

Ten minutes later, demurely wrapped in the primly pretty white cotton robe she'd brought with her, and her hair swathed into a towel, she opened the shutters and stepped outside into the heated shimmer of the day.

She was greeted immediately with a torrent of yapping as Caio, who was lying in the shade of the stone bench, rose to condemn her intrusion.

Laura halted in faint dismay. Up to now, although he was in the adjoining room, he hadn't disturbed her too much with his barking. But she'd assumed that the Signora had taken him with her to the other end of the house to share her sick room vigil. She certainly hadn't bargained for finding him here in sole and aggressive occupation.

'Good dog,' she said without conviction. 'Look, I just want to get my hair dry. There's enough room for us both. Don't give me a hard time, now.'

Still barking, he advanced towards her, then almost jerked to a halt, and she realised he was actually tied to the bench. And, next to where he'd been lying, there was a dish with some dry-looking food on it, and, what was worse, an empty water bowl.

'Oh, for heaven's sake.' She spoke aloud in real anger. Caio would never feature on any 'favourite pets' list of hers, but he deserved better than to be left tied up and thirsty.

She moved round to the other end of the bench, out of the range of his display of sharp teeth, and grabbed the bowl. She took it back to her bathroom, and filled it to the brim with cold water.

When she reappeared, Caio had retreated back under the bench. He growled at her approach, but his heart clearly wasn't in it, and the beady, suspicious eyes were fixed on the bowl. She put it on the ground, then, to demonstrate that the suspicion was mutual, used her hairbrush to push the water near enough for the tethered dog to reach it. He gave a slight whimper, then plunged his muzzle into the bowl, filling the silence with the sound of his frantic lapping.

When he'd finished every drop, he raised his head and looked at her in unmistakable appeal.

I could lose a hand here, Laura thought, but Caio made no attempt to snap as she retrieved the bowl and refilled it for him.

'You poor little devil,' she said gently as he drank again. 'I bet she's forgotten all about you.'

The leash used to tie him was a long one, but Laura realised that it had become twined round the leg of the bench, reducing his freedom considerably.

She could, she thought, untangle it, if he'd let her. But would he allow her close enough to unclip the leash from his collar, without doing her some damage?

Well, she could but try. She certainly couldn't leave him here like this. She could remember hearing once that looking dogs in the eye made them more aggressive, so she seated herself at the far end of the bench, and moved towards him by degrees. When she was in his space, she clenched her hand into a fist and offered it to him, trying to be confident about it, and talking to him quietly at the same time. His initial sniff was reluctant, but he didn't bite, and she tried stroking his head, which he permitted warily.

'You may be spoiled and obnoxious,' she told him, 'but I don't think you have much of a life.'

She slid her fingers down to the ruff of hair round his neck and found his collar. As she released the clip Caio made a sound between a bark and a whimper, and was gone, making for the open space of the garden beyond the courtyard. And after that, presumably, the world.

'Oh, God,' Laura muttered, jumping to her feet and running after him, stumbling a little over the hem of her robe.

What the hell would she do if she couldn't find him? And what was she going to say to the Signora, anyway? She'd be accused of interfering, which was true, and coming back with a counter-accusation of animal negligence, however justified, wouldn't remedy the situation.

She had no idea how extensive the villa's grounds were, or if they were even secure. Supposing he got out onto the mountain itself, and a wolf found him before she could?

This is what happens when you try to be a canine Samaritan, she thought breathlessly as she reached the courtyard entrance, only to find herself almost cannoning into Alessio, who was approaching from the opposite direction with a squirming Caio tucked firmly under his arm.

'Oh, you found him,' she exclaimed. 'Thank heaven for that.'

'I almost fell over him,' he told her tersely. 'Where has he come from?'

'He was tied to the bench over there. I was trying to make him more comfortable, and he just—took off. I was terrified that I wouldn't be able to find him.'

'He was out here—in this heat?' Alessio's tone was incredulous, with the beginnings of anger. He glanced at the bench. 'At least he had water.' He looked at Laura again, more closely. 'Or did he?'

She sighed. 'Well, he has now, and that's what matters.' She was suddenly searingly conscious of the fact that she was wearing nothing but a thin robe, and that her damp hair was hanging on her shoulders. 'I—I'll leave him with you, shall I?' she added, beginning to back away.

'One moment,' he said. 'What made you come out here at this time?'

'I couldn't sleep. I thought I'd wash my hair, and dry it in the sun.' She forced a smile. 'As you see.'

His brows lifted. 'A rather primitive solution, don't you think? Why didn't you ring the bell for Emilia? She would have found you an electric dryer.'

'I felt she had enough on her plate without running around after me. And it is siesta time, after all.' She paused. 'So, why are you here, come to that?'

'I could not sleep either.' He glanced down at Caio, who returned him a baleful look. 'Under the circumstances, that was fortunate.'

'Just in time to spoil his bid for freedom, poor little mutt.' She offered the dog her hand again, and found her fingers being licked by his small rough tongue.

'You seem to have made a friend, *bella mia*.' Alessio sounded amused. 'My aunt will have another reason for jealousy.' He scratched the top of Caio's head. 'And I thought the whole world was his enemy.'

'He'll think so too, if we tie him up to that bench again,' Laura said ruefully.

'Then we will not do so. I will put him in my aunt's room instead, with his water. His basket is there, anyway, and he will be cooler,' he added, frowning. 'I cannot imagine why she would leave him anywhere else.' He sighed. 'Another topic for discussion that will displease her.'

'Another?'

'I have yet to raise the subject of your visit to Paolo.'

'Oh, please,' Laura said awkwardly. 'I've been thinking about that, and maybe I shouldn't persist. If she's so adamant, it will only cause problems.'

He said gently, 'But that is nonsense, Laura *mia*. Of course you must see your lover. Your visit can do nothing but good, I am sure.' His gaze travelled over her, from the high, frilled neck of her robe, down to her bare insteps, and she felt every inch of concealed skin tingle under his lingering regard. Felt an odd heat burgeoning inside her, which had nothing to do with the warmth of the day.

He smiled at her. 'And I will ask Emilia to bring you the hair-dryer,' he added softly, then turned away.

Laura regained the sanctuary of her room, aware that her breathing had quickened out of all proportion.

She closed the shutters behind her, then, on impulse, decided to fasten the small iron bar that locked them. It had clearly not been used for some time because it resisted, finally falling into place with a bang that resounded in the quiet of the afternoon like a pistol shot.

She could only hope Alessio hadn't heard it, because he'd be bound to put two and two together. And the last thing she needed was for him to think that he made her nervous in any way.

Because she had nothing to fear from him, and she was flattering herself to think otherwise.

Someone like Alessio Ramontella would live on a diet of film stars and heiresses, she told herself, pushing her damp hair back from her face with despondent fingers. And if he's kind to me, it's because he recognises I'm out of my depth, and feels sorry for me.

And as long as I remember that, I'm in no danger. No danger at all.

Her reunion with the dying Paolo was scheduled to take place before dinner. A note signed 'Ramontella' informing her of the arrangement had been brought to her by Emilia, along with the promised hair-dryer.

He'd certainly wasted no time over the matter, Laura thought as she followed Guillermo over to the other side of the villa. All she had to do now was pretend to be suitably eager.

She'd dressed for the occasion, putting on her other decent dress, a slim fitting blue shift, sleeveless and scoop-necked. Trying to upgrade it with a handful of silver chains and a matching bracelet.

She'd painted her fingernails and toenails a soft coral, and used a toning lustre on her mouth, emphasising her grey eyes with shadow and kohl.

The kind of effort a girl would make for her lover, she hoped.

She found herself in a long passageway, looking out onto yet another courtyard. The fountain here was larger, she saw, pausing, and a much more elaborate affair, crowned by the statue of a woman crafted in marble. She stood on tiptoe, as if about to take flight, hair and scanty draperies flying behind her, and a bow in her hand, gazing out across the tumbling water that fell from the rock at her feet.

'The goddess Diana for whom the villa is named, *signorina*,' Guillermo, who had halted too, told her in his halting English. 'Very beautiful, *sì*?'

'Very,' Laura agreed with less than total certainty as she studied the remote, almost inhuman face. The virgin huntress, she thought, who unleashed her hounds on any man unwise enough to look at her, and who had the cold moon as her symbol.

And not the obvious choice of deity for someone as overtly warm-blooded as Alessio Ramontella. Her dogs would have torn him to pieces on sight.

She looked down the passage to the tall double doors at the end. 'Is that Signor Paolo's room?'

'But no, *signorina*.' He sounded almost shocked. 'That is the suite of His Excellency. The *signore*, his cousin, is here.' He turned briskly to the left, down another much shorter corridor, and halted, knocking at a door.

It was flung open immediately, and the Signora swept out, her eyes raking Laura with an expression of pure malevolence.

'You may have ten minutes,' she snapped. 'No more. My son needs rest.'

What does she think? Laura asked herself ironically as she entered. That I'm planning to jump his bones?

The shutters were closed and the drapes were drawn too, so the room, which smelled strongly of something like camphorated oil, was lit only by a lamp at the side of the bed.

Paolo was lying, eyes closed, propped up by pillows. He was wearing maroon pyjamas, which made him look sallow, Laura thought. Or maybe it was the effect of the lamplight.

She pulled up a chair, and sat beside the bed. 'Hi,' she said gently. 'How are you feeling?'

'Terrible.' His voice was hoarse and pettish, and the eyes he turned on her were bloodshot and watering. 'Not well enough to talk, but Alessio insisted. I had to listen to him arguing with my mother, and my headache returned. What is it you want?'

'I don't want anything.' She bit her lip. 'Paolo, we're supposed to be crazy about each other, remember? It would seem really weird if I didn't ask for you.' She hesitated. 'I think your cousin feels that I'm stuck here in a kind of vacuum, and feels sorry for me.'

'He would do better to concentrate his compassion on me,' Paolo said sullenly. 'He refuses to call a doctor, although he knows that I have had a weak chest since childhood, and my mother fears this cold may settle there.' He gave a hollow cough as if to prove his point. 'He said he would prefer to summon a vet to examine Caio, and he and my mother quarrelled again.'

Laura sighed. 'I'm sorry if you're having a difficult time, but you're not the only one.' She leaned forward. 'Paolo, I'm finding it really hard to cope with being the uninvited guest round here. I need you to support me—take off some of the pressure.' She paused. 'How long, do you think, before you're well enough to get up and join the real world again?'

'When *Mamma* considers I am out of danger, and not before,' he said, with something of a snap. 'She alone knows how ill I am. She has been wonderful to me—a saint in her patience and care.' He sneezed violently, and lay back, dabbing his nose with a bunch of tissues. 'And my health is more important than your convenience,' he added in a muffled voice.

She got to her feet. She said crisply, 'Actually, it's your own convenience that's being served here. You seem to be overlooking that. But if you'd rather I kept my distance, that's fine with me.'

'I did not mean that,' he said, his tone marginally more conciliatory. 'Of course I wish you to continue to play your part, now more than ever. I shall tell *Mamma* that you must visit me each day—to aid my recovery. That I cannot live without you,' he added with sudden inspiration.

Her mouth tightened. 'No need to go to those lengths, perhaps. But at least it will give me a purpose for staying on.'

'And you can go sightseeing, even if I am not with you,' he went on. 'I shall tell *Mamma* to put Giacomo and the car at your service at once.' He coughed again. 'But now I have talked enough, and my throat is hurting. I need to sleep to become well, you understand.'

'Yes,' she said. 'Of course.' She moved to the door. 'Well— I'll see you tomorrow.'

Outside, she leaned against the wall and drew a deep breath. The daily visits would be a rod for her back, but, to balance that, being able to use the car was an unexpected lifeline.

It offered her a means of escape from the enclosed world of the villa, she thought, and, more vitally, meant that she would no longer be thrown into the company of Alessio Ramontella.

And that was just what she wanted, she told herself. Wasn't it?

CHAPTER SIX

EXCEPT, of course, it had all been too good to be true. As she should probably have known, Laura thought wryly.

Several long days had passed since Paolo had airily promised her the use of the car, and yet she was still confined to the villa and its grounds, with no release in sight.

Naturally, it was the Signora who had applied the veto. Paolo was still far from well, she'd pronounced ominously, and, if there was an emergency, then the car would be needed.

'If you had wished to explore Umbria, *signorina*, then perhaps you should have accepted my nephew's generous invitation,' she'd added, making Laura wonder how she'd come by that particular snippet of information.

But it was an invitation that, signally, had not been repeated, although she often heard the noise of the Jeep driving away.

And far from them being thrown together, after that first day, the Count seemed to have chosen deliberately to remain aloof from her.

He'd finished his breakfast and gone by the time she appeared each morning, but he continued to join her at dinner, although the conversation between them seemed polite and oddly formal compared with their earlier exchanges. And afterwards, he excused himself quickly and courteously, so that she was left strictly to her own devices.

So perhaps he too had sensed the danger of being over-friendly. And, having brought about her reunion with Paolo in spite of his aunt's disapproval, considered his duty done.

She should have found the new regime far less disturbing, and easier to cope with, but somehow it wasn't.

Even in his absence, she was still conscious of him, as if his presence had invaded every stone of the villa's walls. She found she was waiting for his return—listening for his footsteps, and the sound of his voice.

And worst of all was seeing his face in the darkness as she fought restlessly for sleep each night.

The evening meal, she acknowledged wretchedly, was now the highlight of her day, in spite of its new restrictions.

It was an attitude she'd have condemned as ludicrous in anyone else, and she knew it.

And if someone had warned her that she would feel like this, one day, about a man that she hardly even knew, she would not have believed them.

Yet it was happening to her—twenty-first-century Laura. She was trapped, held helpless by the sheer force of her own untried emotions. By feelings that were as old as eternity.

She'd soon discovered that he was not simply on vacation at the villa when she'd made herself take up his invitation to borrow something to read. His library, she saw, was not merely shelved out with books from floor to ceiling, but its vast antique desk was also home to a state-of-the-art computer system, which explained why he was closeted there for much of the time he spent at the villa.

Though not, of course, when she'd paid her visit. It had been Emilia who had waited benignly while she'd made her selection. She had just been hesitating over a couple of modern thrillers, when, to her surprise, she had come on a complete set of Jane Austen, and her choice had been made. She'd glanced through them, appreciating the beautiful leather bindings, then decided on *Mansfield Park*, which she hadn't read since her school days.

The name Valentina Ramontella was inscribed on the flyleaf in an elegant sloping hand, and Emilia, in answer to her tentative enquiry, had told her, with a sigh, that this had been the name of His Excellency's beloved mother, and these books her particular property.

'I see.' Laura touched the signature gently with her forefinger. 'Well, please assure the Count I'll take great care of it.'

However tenuous, it was almost a connection between them, she thought as she took the book away.

But, although the hours seemed strangely empty in Alessio's absence, she was not entirely without companionship as one day stretched endlessly into the next.

Because, to her infinite surprise, Caio had attached himself to her. He was no longer kept in the courtyard, but she'd come across a reluctant Guillermo taking him for a walk in the garden, on the express orders of his master, he'd told her glumly. Seeing his face, and listening to the little dog's excited whimpers as he'd strained on the leash to reach her, Laura had volunteered to take over this daily duty—if the Signora agreed.

Even more surprisingly, permission had been ungraciously granted. And, after a couple of days, Caio trotted beside her so obediently, she dispensed with the leash altogether.

He sometimes accompanied her down to the pool, lying under her sun lounger, and sat beside her in the *salotto* in the evenings as she flexed her rusty fingering on some of the Beethoven sonatas she'd found in bound volumes inside the piano stool. At mealtimes, apart from dinner, he was stationed unobtrusively under her chair, and he'd even joined her on the bed for siesta on a couple of occasions, she admitted guiltily.

'I see you have acquired a bodyguard,' was Alessio's only comment when he encountered them together once, delivered with a faint curl of the mouth.

Watching him walk away, she scooped Caio defensively into her arms. 'We're just a couple of pariahs here,' she murmured to him, and he licked her chin almost wistfully.

But she never took Caio to Paolo's room, instinct telling this would be too much for the Signora, who had no idea of the scope of her pet's defection to the enemy.

And I don't want her to know, Laura thought grimly. I'm unpopular enough already. I don't want to be accused of pinching her dog.

On his own admission, Paolo's cold symptoms had all but vanished, but he refused to leave his room on the grounds that he was still suffering with his chest.

Laura realised that her impatience with him and her ambiguous situation was growing rapidly and would soon reach snapping point.

These ten-minute stilted visits each evening wouldn't convince anyone that they were sharing a grand passion, she thought with exasperated derision. And if the Signora was listening at the door, she'd be justified in wagering her diamonds that she'd soon have Beatrice Manzone as a daughter-in-law.

But: 'You worry too much,' was Paolo's casual response to her concern.

Well, if he was satisfied, then why should she quibble? she thought with an inward shrug. He was the paying customer, after all. And found herself grimacing at the thought.

But as she left his room that evening the Signora was waiting for her, her lips stretched in the vinegary smile first encountered in Rome. Still, any calibre of smile was a welcome surprise, Laura thought, tension rising within her.

She was astonished to be told that, as Giacomo would be driving to the village the next morning to collect some special medicine from the pharmacy, she was free to accompany him there, if she wished.

'You may have some small errands, *signorina*.' The older woman's shrug emphasised their trifling quality. 'But the medicine is needed, so you will not be able to remain for long.'

Well, it was better than nothing, Laura thought, offering a polite word of thanks instead of the cartwheel she felt like turning. In fact, it was almost a 'get out of jail' card.

Saved, she thought, with relief. Saved from cabin fever, and, hopefully, other obsessions too.

She'd have time to buy some postcards at least—let her family know she was still alive. And Gaynor, too, would be waiting to hear from her.

In the morning, she was ready well before the designated time, anxious that Giacomo would have no excuse to set off without her. She still couldn't understand why the Signora should suddenly be so obliging, and couldn't help wondering if the older woman was playing some strange game of cat and mouse with her.

But that makes no sense, she adjured herself impatiently. Don't start getting paranoid.

Seated in the front, Laura kept her eyes fixed firmly ahead as the car negotiated the winding road down to the valley, avoiding any chance glimpse of the mind-aching drop on one side, and praying that they would meet no other vehicles coming from the opposite direction.

She only realised when the descent was completed that she'd been holding her breath most of the time.

Giacomo drove straight to the main square, and parked near the church. Pointing to the hands on his watch, he conveyed that she had fifteen minutes only to spend in Besavoro, and Laura nodded in resigned acceptance.

Well, that was the deal, she told herself philosophically as she set off. And she would just have to make the most of it.

She soon realised that Besavoro was in reality a small town, and not what she thought of as a village at all. The square was lined with shops, selling every sort of food, as well as wine, olive oil, hardware and clothing. It all had a busy, purposeful air, without a designer boutique or gift shop in sight.

But the little news agency she came to sold a few postcards, featuring mainly Assisi and the Majella national park, and she bought four, deciding to send one to Carl, her immediate boss at Harman Grace as well.

No one in the shop spoke English, but with great goodwill the correct stamps for Britain were offered, and her change was counted carefully into her hand.

A few doors away was a bar with tables on the pavement, and Laura took a seat, ordering a coffee and a bottle of mineral water.

She glanced across the square, checking the car, and then, carefully, her watch, before starting to write her cards.

At the same time she was aware that people were checking her, not rudely, but with open interest. English tourists were clearly a rarity here, she realised, turning her own attention back to the task in hand.

She was sorely tempted to put, 'Having ghastly time. Glad you're not here,' but knew that would involve her in impossible

explanations on her return. Better, she decided, to stick to the
usual anodyne messages. To Gaynor alone could she eventually
reveal the grisly truth, and wait for her to say, 'I told you so,'
she thought ruefully.

Although there were things about her stay at the villa that she
wasn't prepared to talk about—ever. Not even to Gaynor.

Now all she needed was a postbox, she thought, rifling through
her small phrase book for the exact wording. On the other hand
it was probably quicker and easier to ask Giacomo.

She slipped her pen back into her bag, and felt for her purse,
looking again towards the church as she did so.

But where the car had stood only minutes before, there was
an empty space.

Laura shot to her feet with a stifled cry of dismay. It couldn't
have gone, she thought wildly. There were still minutes to spare.
And if Giacomo had just looked across the square he'd have seen
her. So why hadn't he come across to her—or sounded his horn
even? Why—simply drive off?

The bar owner came dashing out, clearly worried that she was
about to do a runner, his voice raised in protest.

Laura pointed. 'My lift—it's vanished. I—I'm stranded.'

The owner spread his hands in total incomprehension, talking
excitedly. She became aware that people were pausing—staring.
Beginning to ask questions. Hemming her in as they did so.
Making her uncomfortably aware of her sudden isolation, in a
strange country, and unable to speak a word of the language.

Then, suddenly, across the increasing hubbub, cut a drawl she
recognised. '*Ciao, bella mia.* Having problems?'

Alessio had come through the small crowd, which had obediently parted for him, and was standing just a couple of feet
away, watching her from behind dark glasses, hands on hips. The
shorts he was wearing today were marginally more decent than
the first pair she'd seen him in, but his dark blue shirt was unbuttoned almost to the waist.

And if she was pleased to see him, she was determined that
he wasn't going to know it.

She faced him furiously. 'Actually—yes. The damned car's

gone without me.' She almost stamped her foot, but decided against it. 'Oh, God, I don't believe it.' She bit her lip. 'I suppose this is your aunt's idea—to make me walk back up that hill, in the hope I'll die of heatstroke.'

He grinned. 'Calm yourself, Laura. This time Zia Lucrezia is innocent. I told Giacomo to return to the villa.'

'But why?' She stared at him. 'There was no need. We had a perfectly good arrangement...'

Alessio shrugged. 'I felt you needed a break. Also, that Besavoro deserved more than just fifteen minutes of your time. Was I so wrong?'

'Well, no,' she conceded without pleasure.

'Good,' he approved lazily. 'And when you have completed your sightseeing, I will drive you back in the Jeep.'

Laura suddenly realised that public interest in her activities had snowballed since the Count's arrival. The fascinated circle gathering around them was now three deep.

She said stiffly, 'I thought I'd made it clear. I don't want you to put yourself to any trouble on my behalf.'

'There is no trouble—except perhaps with Luigi here.' He indicated the gaping bar owner. 'So, why don't you sit down and finish your drink before he has a fit, hmm?'

He turned to the nearest onlooker, and said something softly. As if a switch had been pressed, the crowd began to melt unobtrusively away.

Such is power, Laura thought mutinously as she obeyed. She watched him drop into the chair opposite, stretching long tanned legs out in front of him as he ordered another cappuccino for Laura, and an espresso for himself from Luigi.

He'd caught her totally on the back foot, she thought. And she resented that swift painful thud of the heart that his unexpected appearance had engendered. Especially when he'd practically ignored her for the past week.

But I should want to be ignored, she thought. I should want to be totally ostracised by him. Because it's safer that way...

'Please do not let me interrupt.' He nodded to the small pile of cards. 'Finish your correspondence.'

'I already have done.' She smiled over-brightly. 'Just touching base with family and friends.'

'Ah,' he said. 'The family that, according to my aunt, does not exist.'

Laura groaned inwardly. Paolo had reacted with ill temper to her confession that she'd deviated from the party line.

She made herself shrug. 'I can't imagine where she got that idea. Perhaps it suited her better to believe that I was a penniless orphan.'

'Which, of course, you are not.'

'Well, the penniless bit is fairly accurate. It's been a real struggle for my mother since my father died. I'm just glad I've got a decent job, so that I can help.'

The dark brows lifted. 'Does working in a wine bar pay so well? I did not know.'

But that's not the day job. The words hovered on her lips, but, thankfully, remained unspoken.

Oh, God, she thought, hastily marshalling her thoughts. I've goofed again.

She met his sardonic gaze. 'It's a busy place, *signore*, and the tips are good.'

'Ah,' he said softly. He glanced around him. 'So, what are your impressions of Besavoro?'

'It's larger than I thought, and much older. I didn't think I would catch more than a glimpse of it, of course.'

'I thought you would be pleased that I sent Giacomo away for another reason,' he said, leaning back in his chair, and pushing his sunglasses up onto his forehead. 'It will mean that Paolo will get his medicine more quickly, and maybe return to your arms, *subito*, a man restored.'

'I doubt it.' She looked down at the table. 'He seems set for the duration.' She hesitated. 'Has he always fussed about his health like this? I mean—he's simply got a cold.'

'Why, Laura,' he said softly. 'How hard you are. For a man, no cold is ever simple.'

'Well, I can't imagine you going to bed for a week.'

'No?' His smile was wicked. The dark eyes seemed to graze

her body. 'Then perhaps you need to extend the scope of your imagination, *mia cara*.'

I am not—*not* going to blush, Laura told herself silently. And I don't care how much he winds me up.

She looked back at him squarely, 'I meant—with some minor ailment, *signore*.'

'Perhaps not.' He shrugged. 'But my temper becomes so evil, I am sure those around me wish I would retire to my room—and stay there until I can be civil again.'

He paused while Luigi placed the coffees in front of them. 'But I have to admit that Paolo was a sickly child, and I think his mother plays on this, by pampering him, and making him believe every cough and sneeze is a serious threat. It is her way of retaining some hold on him.'

'I'm sure of it,' Laura said roundly. 'I suspect Beatrice Manzone has had a lucky escape.' And could have bitten her tongue out again as Alessio's gaze sharpened.

'Davvero?' he queried softly. 'A curious point of view to have about your *innamorato*, perhaps.'

'I meant,' Laura said hastily, in a bid to retrieve the situation, 'that I shan't be as submissive—or as easy to manipulate—as she would have been.'

'Credo,' he murmured, his mouth twisting. 'I believe you, *mia cara*. You have that touch of red in your hair that spells danger.'

He picked up his cup. 'Now, drink your coffee, and I will take you to see the church,' he added more briskly. 'There is a Madonna and Child behind the high altar that some people say was painted by Raphael.'

'But you don't agree?' Laura welcomed the change of direction.

He considered, frowning a little. 'I think it is more likely to have been one of his pupils. For one thing, it is unsigned, and Raphael liked to leave his mark. For another, Besavoro is too unimportant to appeal to an artist of his ambition. And lastly the Virgin does not resemble Raphael's favourite mistress, whom he is said to have used as his chief model, even for the Sistine Madonna.'

'Wow,' Laura said, relaxing into a smile. 'How very sacrilegious of him.'

He grinned back at her. 'I prefer to think—what proof of his passion.' He gave a faint shrug. 'But ours is still a beautiful painting, and can be treasured as such.'

He drank the rest of his coffee, and stood up, indicating the postcards. 'You wish me to post these? Before we visit the church?'

'Well, yes.' She hesitated. 'But you don't have to come with me, *signore*. After all, I can hardly get lost. And I know how busy you are. I'm sure you have plenty of other things to do.'

'Perhaps,' he said. 'But today, *mia cara*, I shall devote to you.' His smile glinted. 'Or did you think I had forgotten about you these past days?'

'I—I didn't think anything at all,' she denied hurriedly.

'I am disappointed,' he said lightly. 'I hoped you might have missed me a little.'

'Then maybe you should remember something.' She lifted her chin. 'I came to Besavoro with your cousin, *signore*.'

'Ah,' Alessio said softly. 'But that is so fatally easy to forget, Laura *mia*.'

And he walked off across the square.

The interior of the church was dim, and fragrant with incense. It felt cool, too, after the burning heat of the square outside.

There were a number of small streets, narrow and cobbled, opening off the square, their houses facing each other so closely that people could have leaned from the upper-storey windows and touched, and Laura explored them all.

The shuttered windows suggested a feeling of intimacy, she thought. A sense of busy lives lived in private. And the flowers that spilled everywhere from troughs and window boxes added to Besavoro's peace and charm.

'So,' Alessio said as they paused for some water at a drinking fountain before visiting the church. 'Do you like my town?'

'It's enchanting,' Laura returned with perfect sincerity, smiling inwardly at his casual use of the possessive. The lord, she thought, with his fiefdom. 'A little gem.'

'*Sì,*' he agreed. 'And now I will show you another. *Avanti.*'

Laura trod quietly up the aisle of the church, aware of Alessio following silently. The altar itself was elaborate with gold leaf, but she hardly gave it a second glance. Because, above it, the painting glowed like a jewel, creating its own light.

The girl in it was very young, her hair uncovered, her blue cloak thrown back. She held the child proudly high in her arms, her gaze steadfast, and almost defiant, as if challenging the world to throw the first stone.

Laura caught her breath. She turned to Alessio, eyes shining, her hand going out to him involuntarily. 'It's—wonderful.'

'Yes,' he returned quietly, his fingers closing round hers. 'Each time I see it, I find myself—amazed.'

They stood in silence for a few minutes longer, then, as if by tacit consent, turned and began to walk around the shadowy church, halting briefly at each shrine with its attendant bank of burning candles.

Laura knew she should free her hand, but his warm grasp seemed unthreatening enough. And she certainly didn't want to make something out of nothing, especially in a church, so she allowed her fingers to remain quietly in his.

But as they emerged into the sunshine he let her go anyway. Presumably, thought Laura, the Count Ramontella didn't wish 'his' citizens to see him walking hand in hand with a girl.

Or not my kind of girl, certainly, she amended silently.

She'd expected to be driven straight back to the villa, but to her uneasy surprise Alessio took another road altogether, climbing the other side of the valley.

'Where are we going?' she asked.

'There's a view I wish to show you,' he said. 'It belongs to a *trattoria*, so we can enjoy it over lunch.'

'But aren't we expected back at the villa?'

'You are so keen to return?' He slanted a smile at her. 'You think, maybe, that Paolo's medicine has already worked its magic?'

'No,' she said stiffly. 'Just wondering what your aunt will think.'

'It is only lunch,' he said. The smile lingered—hardened a little. 'And I do not think she will have any objection—or none that need trouble either of us.'

The *trattoria* was a former farmhouse, extensively renovated only a couple of years earlier. Among the improvements had been a long wide terrace, with a thatched roof to provide shade, which overlooked the valley.

Their welcome was warm, but also, Laura noticed, respectful, and they were conducted to a table at the front of the terrace. Menus were produced and they were offered an *aperitivo*.

Laura found herself leaning beside Alessio on the parapet of the broad stone wall, holding a glass of white wine, and looking down onto an endless sea of green, distantly punctuated by the blue ribbon of the river and the dusty thread of the road.

On the edge of her vision, she could see the finger of stone that was Besavoro's *campanile* rising from the terracotta roofs around it.

Higher up, the crags looked almost opalescent in the shimmer of the noonday sun, while on the opposite side of the valley, almost hidden by the clustering forest, she could just make out the sprawl of greyish pink stone that formed the Villa Diana.

She said softly, 'It's—unbelievable. Thank you for showing it to me.'

'The pleasure is mine,' he returned. 'It is a very small world, this valley, but important to me.'

She played with the stem of her glass. 'Yet you must have so many worlds, *signore*.'

'And some I prefer to others.' He paused. 'So, where is your world, Laura? The real one?'

Her tone was stilted. 'London, I guess—for the time being anyway. My work is there.'

'But surely you could work anywhere you wished? Wine bars are not confined to your capital. But I suppose you wish to remain for Paolo's sake.'

She had a sudden longing to tell him the truth. To turn to him and say, 'Actually I work for the PR company your bank has just hired. The wine bar is moonlighting, and Harman Grace would probably have a fit if they knew. Nor am I involved with Paolo. He's renting me as his pretend girlfriend to convince his mother that he won't marry Beatrice Manzone.'

But she couldn't say any such thing, of course, because she'd given Paolo her word.

Instead she said, 'Also, I'm flat-hunting with some friends. We all want to move on from our current grotty bedsits, especially Gaynor and myself, so we thought we'd pool our resources.'

'Does Paolo approve of this plan?' Alessio traced the shape of one of the parapet's flat stones with his finger. 'Won't he wish you to live with him?'

She bit her lip. 'Perhaps—ultimately. I—I don't know. It's too soon for that kind of decision.'

'But this holiday could have been the first step towards it.' There was an odd, almost harsh note in his voice. 'My poor Laura. If so, how cruel to keep you in separate rooms, as I have done.'

She forced a smile. 'Not really. The Signora would have had a fit and I—I might have caught Paolo's cold.'

His mouth twisted. 'A practical thought, *carissima.*' He straightened. 'Now, shall we decide what to eat?'

A pretty, smiling girl, who turned out to be the owner's wife, brought a bowl of olive oil to their table, and a platter of bread to dip into it. The cooking, Alessio explained, was being done by her husband. Then came a dish of Parma ham, accompanied by a bewildering array of sausages, which was followed up by wild boar pâté.

The main course was chicken, simply roasted and bursting with flavour, all of it washed down with a jug of smoky red wine, made, Alessio told her, from the family's own vineyard in Tuscany.

But Laura demurred at the idea of dessert or cheese, raising laughing hands in protest.

'They'll be charging me excess weight on the flight home at this rate.'

Alessio drank some wine, the dark eyes watching her over the top of his glass. 'Maybe you need to gain a little,' he said. 'A man likes to know that he has his woman in his arms. He does not wish her to slip through his fingers like water. Has Paolo never told you so?'

She looked down at the table. 'Not in so many words. And I don't think it's a very fashionable point of view, not in London, anyway.'

The mention of Paolo's name brought her down to earth with a jolt. It had been such a wonderful meal. She'd felt elated—euphoric even—here, above the tops of the trees.

I could reach up a hand, she thought, and touch the sky.

And this, she knew, was entirely because of the man seated across the table from her. The man who somehow had the power to make her forget everything—including the sole reason that had brought her to Italy in the first place.

Stupid, she castigated herself. Eternally, ridiculously stupid to hanker after what she could never have in a thousand years.

Because there was far more than just a table dividing them, and she needed to remember that in her remaining days at the Villa Diana.

Apart from anything else, they'd been acquainted with each other for only a week, which was a long time in politics, but in no other sense.

So how was it that she felt she'd known him all her life? she asked herself, and sighed inwardly. That, of course, was the secret of his success—especially with women.

And her best plan was to escape while she could, and before she managed to make an even bigger fool of herself than she had already.

She was like a tiny planet, she thought, circling the sun, when any slight change in orbit could draw her to self-destruction. Burning up for all eternity.

That cannot happen, she told herself. And I won't let it.

He said, 'A moment ago, you were here with me. Now you have gone.' He leaned forward, his expression quizzical.

'''When, Madonna, will you ever drop that veil you wear in shade and sun?'''

She looked back at him startled. 'I don't understand.'

'I was quoting,' he said. 'From Petrarch—one of his sonnets to Laura. My own translation. It seemed—appropriate.'

She tried to speak lightly. 'You amaze me, *signore*. I never thought I'd hear you speaking poetry.'

He shrugged. 'But I'm sure you could recite from Shakespeare, if I asked you. Am I supposed to have less education?'

'No,' she said quickly. 'No, of course not. I'm sorry. After all, we're strangers. I shouldn't make any assumptions about you.'

He paused. 'Besides, the question is a valid one. Because you also disappear behind a veil sometimes, so that I cannot tell what you're thinking.'

She laughed rather weakly. 'I'm—relieved to hear it.'

'So I shall ask a direct question. What are you hiding, Laura?'

Her fingers twined together in her lap. 'I think as well as a good education, *signore*, you have a vivid imagination.'

He studied her for a moment, his mouth wry. 'And you still will not call me Alessio.'

'Because I don't think it's necessary,' she retorted. 'Or even very wise, you being who you are. Not just a count, but Chairman of the Arleschi Bank.'

'You could not put that out of your mind for a while?'

'No.' Her fingers tightened round each other. 'That's not possible. Besides, I'll be gone soon, anyway.'

'But you forget, *signorina*,' he said silkily. 'You are to become a member of my family. We shall be cousins.'

She paused for a heartbeat. 'Well, when we are,' she said, 'I'll think again about your name.' She gave him a bright smile. 'And now will you take me back to the villa, please? Paolo may need me,' she added for good measure.

As he rose to his feet he was laughing. 'Well, run while you may, my little hypocrite,' he told her mockingly. 'But remember this: you cannot hide—or not for ever.' His fingers stroked her face from the high cheekbone to the corner of her mouth, then he turned and walked away across the terrace to the restaurant's

main door, leaving Laura to stare uneasily after him, her heart
and mind locked into a combat that offered no prospect of peace.
And which, she suddenly knew, could prove mortal.

But only to me, she whispered to herself in swift anguish. Only
to me...

CHAPTER SEVEN

THE return journey was conducted mainly in silence. Laura was occupied with her own troubling thoughts, while Alessio was reviewing the events of the morning with a sense of quiet satisfaction.

She had missed him, he thought. Everything—including all the things she had not said—had betrayed it. So his ploy of keeping aloof from her had succeeded. And, now, she was desperately trying to reinforce her own barricades against him.

But it won't work, *carissima*, he told her silently.

After he'd got rid of Giacomo that morning, he'd stood for a while, watching her from the other side of the square.

She might not have the flamboyant looks of a woman like Vittoria, but her unselfconscious absorption as she wrote gave an impression of peace and charm that he had never encountered before.

And her hair had been truly glorious in the sunlight, the colour of English leaves in autumn. He'd found himself suddenly longing to see it spread across his pillow, so that he could run his fingers through its soft masses and breathe their fragrance.

Also, he'd noted, with additional pleasure, she was again wearing the dress that had so fired his imagination at their first meeting.

And soon, he thought, as he turned the Jeep onto the road up to the villa—soon his fantasies would all be realised.

Not that it would be easy, he mentally amended with sudden restiveness. She might have let him take her hand for a while without protest, but, in many ways, she still continued to elude him, and not just in the physical sense either.

Her relationship with his cousin was certainly an enigma. He didn't particularly share his aunt's opinion that the pair were in

94

love and planning immediate marriage. But then, he admitted, he'd hardly seen them together. Although, that first evening, he'd observed that the little Laura had not seemed to relish her lover's advances. But that might have been because she preferred privacy for such exchanges, and not a family dinner.

Well, privacy she should have, he promised himself, smiling inwardly, and his entire undivided attention as well.

However, he still wondered if, given time, the whole Paolo affair might have withered and died of its own accord, and without Zia Lucrezia's interference.

Not that he'd been able to convince her of that, although he had tried. She'd simply snapped that she could not afford to be patient, and that Paolo's engagement to the Manzone girl must be concluded without further delay.

She'd added contemptuously that the English girl was nothing more than a money-grubbing trollop who deserved to be sent packing in disgrace for attempting to connect herself, even distantly, to the Ramontella family.

'And your part in all this should have been played by now,' she added angrily. 'You should have spent more time with the little fool.'

'I know what I'm doing,' he returned coldly. 'Precisely because the girl is far from a fool, or any of the other names you choose to call her.'

How, in the name of God, could he feel so protective, he asked himself ruefully, afterwards, when he might be planning the possible ruin of Laura's life? If, indeed, it turned out that she cared for Paolo after all.

But on one thing he was totally determined. When he took her, it would be out of their mutual desire alone, and not to placate his aunt. That, he told himself, would be the least of his considerations.

He could salve his conscience to that extent.

And, if humanly possible, it would happen well away from the Villa Diana, and Zia Lucrezia's inevitable and frankly indecent gloating.

Because he needed to make very sure that Laura would never know how they'd been manipulated into each other's arms.

Although that was no longer strictly true—or not for him, anyway, he reminded himself wryly. On his side, at least, the need was genuine, and had been so almost from the first. She was the one who required the persuasion.

Staying away from her over the past few days had been sheer torment, he admitted, to his own reluctant surprise. She had been constantly in the forefront of his mind, waking and sleeping, while his entire body ached intolerably for her too.

He was not accustomed, he acknowledged sardonically, to waiting for a woman. In his world, it was not often that he found it necessary. And it would make her ultimate surrender even more enjoyable.

He cast a lightning sideways glance at her, and saw that her hands were clenched tightly in her lap.

He said lightly, 'Is it the road or my driving that so alarms you, Laura?'

She turned her head, forcing a smile. 'It's the road, although I'm trying to get used to it. We don't have so many death-defying drops in East Anglia, where I come from.'

'Try not to worry too much, *mia bella*.' His tone was dry. 'Believe that I have a vested interest in staying alive.'

There was a movement at the side of the road ahead, and Alessio leaned forward, his gaze sharpening as a stocky, white-haired man wearing overalls came into view, carrying a tall cane shaped like a shepherd's crook. 'Ah,' he said, half to himself. 'Fredo.' He drew the Jeep into the side of the road, and stopped. 'Will you forgive me, *cara*, if I speak to him again about moving down to Besavoro? He has been avoiding me, I think.'

Laura sat in the Jeep and watched with some amusement. The old man stood like a rock, leaning on his cane, occasionally moving his head in quiet negation as Alessio prowled round in front of him talking rapidly in his own language, his hands gesturing urgently in clear appeal.

When at last he paused for breath, the old man reached up and clapped him on the shoulder, his wrinkled face breaking into a smile. Then they talked together for a few more minutes before Fredo turned away, making his slow way up a track on the hillside, and Alessio came back to the Jeep, frowning.

'Still no luck?' she asked.

'He makes his own goats seem reasonable.' He started the engine. 'Also, he says that the weather is going to change. That we shall have storms,' he added, his frown deepening.

Laura looked up at the cloudless sky. 'It doesn't seem like it,' she objected.

'Fredo is rarely wrong about these things. But it will not be for a day—perhaps two.' He slanted a smile at her. 'So make the most of the sun while you can.'

'I've been doing just that.' She paused. 'In fact,' she went on hesitantly, 'I was—concerned in case I'd kept you away from the pool. If you preferred to have it to yourself. Because I've noticed that you—you haven't been swimming for a while.'

'I swim every day,' he said. 'But very early. Before breakfast, when there is no one else about, but that is not through any wish to avoid your company, *mia bella*, but because I like to swim naked.'

'Oh.' Laura swallowed. 'Oh, I—I understand. Of course.'

'Although,' he went on softly, 'you could always join me if you wished. The water feels wonderful at that time of day.'

'I'm sure it does,' Laura said woodenly, all sorts of forbidden images leaping to mind. 'But I think I'll stick to my own timetable. *Grazie*,' she added politely.

'*Prego,*' he returned, and she could hear the laughter in his voice.

Furiously aware that her face had warmed, Laura relapsed into a silence that lasted until their arrival at the villa.

As she left the Jeep she thanked Alessio for the lunch in the tone of a polite schoolgirl taking leave of a favourite uncle, and went off to her room, trying not to look as if she was escaping.

Her clothes were clinging to her in the heat, so she stripped quickly and took a cool shower. Then, she put on her robe and lay down on the bed, trying to relax. But her mind was still teeming with thoughts and impressions from the morning.

It was weird, she thought, that Alessio—the Count, she amended hastily—should just turn up like that, out of the blue. And even more disturbing that she should have enjoyed being with him quite so much.

She'd been unnerved too by his suggestion that she was hiding something. He might have dressed it up in poetic language about veils, she thought ruefully, but basically he was issuing a warning that he was on to her.

And in turn she would have to warn Paolo, on her evening visit, that his lordly cousin was growing suspicious.

She found herself sighing a little. These visits were becoming more problematic each time. Quite apart from his obsession about his cold, it was difficult to hold a conversation with someone she hardly knew, and with whom she barely had a thought in common, especially when she suspected his mother was listening at the door.

I wish all this had never happened, she told herself vehemently. That I'd never agreed to this ridiculous pretence. And, most of all, that I'd never come here and set eyes on Count Ramontella. Better for me that he'd just remained a name on a letterhead.

Easy to say, she thought, but did she really mean it? Would she truly have wanted to live her life without having experienced this frankly dangerous encounter? Without having felt the lure of his smile, or reacting to the teasing note in his voice? Without realising, dry-mouthed, that he had simply—entered the room?

No, she thought sadly. If I'm honest, I wouldn't have wanted to miss one precious moment with him. But now the situation's getting altogether trickier, and I really need to distance myself. Put the width of Europe between us, and become sane again.

It's safer that way, and I'm a safety-conscious girl. I have to be.

She sighed again. Alessio Ramontella was just a dream to take back with her to mundane reality, she thought wistfully. A private fantasy to lighten up her fairly staid existence. And that was all he ever would, or could be...

Until one day, when he would become nothing but a fading

memory. And she could relax, lower her guard, and get on with her own life.

Perhaps, in time, she might even convince herself that none of this had ever happened.

She sat up, swinging her legs to the floor. She was obviously not going to sleep, so she might take the Count's advice, and exploit the fine weather while it persisted.

She changed swiftly into her swimsuit, slipped on the filmy voile shirt she used as a cover-up, and went down to the pool.

As she reached the bottom of the steps she was disconcerted to see that she would not be alone that afternoon either. That Alessio was there before her, stretched out on a lounger, reading.

He seemed deeply absorbed, and Laura hesitated, wondering if she should turn quietly and make a strategic withdrawal before she was noticed. But it was already too late for that, because he was putting down his book and getting to his feet in one lithe movement, the sculpted mouth smiling faintly as he looked at her.

'So you came after all,' he said softly. 'I had begun to wonder.'

'I—I decided to take your friend at his word.' She paused. 'I hope I'm not disturbing you.'

He said lightly, 'Not in any way that you think, *mia cara.*' He moved a lounger into the shade of a parasol for her, and arranged the cushions.

'Thank you.' She felt self-conscious enough to have stood on one leg and sucked her thumb. And he'd placed her sunbed far too close to his own, she thought with misgiving. However, it seemed unwise to make any kind of fuss, so she walked across and sat down, forcing a smile as she looked up at him. 'Heavens, it's hotter than ever.'

'Yes.' Alessio glanced up at the mountains with a slight frown. 'I begin to think Fredo may be right.'

Laura reached down and retrieved his book, which had slipped off his lounger onto the marble tiles between them. 'Francesco Petrarca' was emblazoned in faded gilt letters across its leather cover.

'Reading more poetry about veiled ladies, *signore*?' She

handed it to him. Literature, she thought. Now there's a safe topic for conversation.

'There is much to read,' he said drily. 'The great Francesco made his Laura's name a song for twenty years.'

'How did they meet?'

'He saw her,' Alessio said, after a pause. 'Saw her one day, and fell in love for ever.'

'And did they live happily ever after?'

'They lived their own lives, but not together. She—belonged to another man.'

She made a thing of adjusting her sunglasses. She said lightly, 'Then maybe he shouldn't have allowed himself to fall in love.'

'Ah,' he said softly. 'But perhaps, Laura *mia*, he could not help himself. Listen.' He found a page, and read aloud. '"I was left defenceless against love's attack, with no barrier between my eyes and my heart."'

He put the book down. 'Is there a defence against love, I wonder?' The dark gaze seemed to bore into hers. 'What do you think, *bella mia*? Did Paolo travel straight from your eyes to your heart when you saw him first?'

No, she thought, pain twisting inside her. But you did—and now I'm lost for ever...

She made herself look back at him. 'Naturally there was—a connection. Why else would I be here?'

'Why indeed?' he said softly. He stretched slowly, effortlessly, making her numbly aware of every smooth ripple of muscle in his lean body. 'I am going to swim, Laura. Will you join me?'

'No,' she managed somehow. 'No, thank you.'

He smiled at her. 'You do not feel the necessity to cool off a little?'

'I'm a very poor swimmer,' she said. 'I don't like being out of my depth, and your pool has no shallow end.'

'Ah,' he said meditatively. 'Then why do you not allow me to teach you?'

There was a loaded silence, and Laura found she was biting her lip. 'That's—very kind,' she said, trying to keep her voice steady. 'But I couldn't—possibly—impose on you like that.'

'No imposition, *cara mia.*' His voice was a drawl. 'It would be my privilege, and my pleasure. Besides,' he added with faint reproof, 'everyone should be able to swim safely. Don't you agree?'

'I—I suppose so.' Except that we're not really talking about swimming, she thought wildly, and we both know it. So why—why are you doing this?

He said softly, 'But you are not convinced.' He walked to the far end of the pool, and dived in, swimming the whole length under water. He surfaced, shaking the water from his hair, and swam slowly to the edge, resting his arms on the tiled surround.

He beckoned. 'Laura, come to me.' He spoke quietly, but the imperative came over loud and clear. She realised, not for the first time, why he was a force to be reckoned with within the Arleschi Bank.

Reluctantly, she shed the voile shirt and walked over to the edge of the pool, reed-slender in her green swimsuit.

She said coolly, 'Do you always expect to be obeyed, *signore*?'

'Always.' The sun glistened on the dark hair as he looked up at her. He added softly, 'But I prefer compliance to submission, *signorina.*' He paused, allowing her to assimilate that, then smiled. 'Now sit on the edge,' he directed. 'Put your hands on my arms, and lower yourself into the water. I promise I will keep you safe.'

Her heart juddered. Oh, but it's too late, she thought. Much too late for that.

But she did as she was told, gasping as the coolness of the water made contact with her overheated skin, aware of Alessio's hands, firm as rocks, under her elbows.

'You can stand,' she accused breathlessly. 'But I can't reach. I'm treading water.'

'Then do so,' he said. 'You will come to no harm.' He added with faint amusement, 'And I can do nothing about the disparity in our heights, *bella mia.*'

He paused. 'You say you can swim a little?' And, when she

nodded without much conviction, 'The width of the pool, perhaps?'

'Possibly,' Laura said with dignity. She hesitated. 'But not
without touching the bottom with my toe,' she conceded unwill-
ingly.

He sighed. 'Then the true answer is no,' he commented aus-
terely. 'So, we shall begin.'

It was one of the strangest hours of her life. If she'd imagined
Alessio had lured her into the pool for his own dubious purposes,
then she had to think again and quickly, because his whole attitude was brisk, almost impersonal. He really intended to teach
her to swim, she realised in astonishment as she struggled to co-
ordinate her arm and leg movements and her breathing, while his
hand cupped her chin.

One of her problems, he told her, was her apparent reluctance
to put her face in the water.

'What does it matter if your make-up is spoiled?' he said.

'I'm not wearing make-up,' she retorted, trying to catch her
breath.

He slanted a faint grin at her. 'I know. Now let us try again.

'You lack confidence, no more than that, so you must learn to
trust the water,' he directed eventually. 'Let it hold you, and do
not fight it. Now, turn on your back and float for a while. I will
support you.'

She did as she was bidden, feeling the dazzle of the sun on
her closed eyelids.

She was not even aware of the moment he gently withdrew
his hand from beneath her head until she heard him say, '*Brava*,
Laura. You do well,' and realised he was no longer beside her.

Her eyes flew open in swift panic, to see him watching her
from the side of the pool, and she floundered suddenly, coughing
and spluttering. He reached her in a moment, and held her.

'You let go of me,' she gasped.

'About five minutes ago,' he told her drily. 'You stopped be-
lieving. That is all. But now, when you are ready, you will swim
beside me across the pool, because you know you can. And remember to breathe,' he added sternly.

She gave him a mutinous look. '*Sì, signore.*'

But to her amazement she did it, and she felt almost euphoric with achievement when she found herself clinging to the opposite edge, catching her breath.

Alessio pulled himself out of the water, and stood for a moment, raking back his wet hair. Then he bent, sliding his hands under Laura's armpits, lifting her out to join him as if she were a featherweight.

'But I wanted to swim back,' she objected, smiling up at him as he put her down on the tiles.

'I think that is enough for the first time,' he said softly. He paused. 'After all, I do not wish to exhaust you.' His hands moved slowly to her shoulders. Remained there.

Laura was suddenly aware of a strange stillness as if the world had halted on its axis. Or was it just that her heart seemed to have stopped beating? He had told her to breathe, she thought confusedly, but it was impossible. Her throat was too tight.

In spite of the heat, she was shivering, an unfamiliar weakness penetrating the pit of her stomach.

He was looking down at her, she realised, watching her parted lips. He was smiling a little, but there was no laughter in the half-closed eyes, which studied her with frank intensity, as if mesmerised.

He bent towards her, and she thought, He's going to kiss me.

Deep within her, she felt a pang of yearning so acute that the stifled breath burst from her in a raw, shocked gasp. And with it came a kind of sanity as she realised exactly what she was inviting. And from whom...

She heard a voice she barely recognised as her own say raggedly, 'No—Alessio—please, no!'

The dark brows lifted wryly. He reached up, and framed her face with both hands, his thumbs stroking back the wet strands of hair behind her ears, then stroking gently along her cheekbones and down to the fragility of her jawline.

She felt him touch the corners of her quivering mouth, then the long fingers travelled down her throat to her shoulders again.

He said softly, 'No?'

He hooked a finger under the strap of her swimsuit, and drew it down, then bent, brushing his lips softly across the faint mark it had left on her skin.

Laura felt her whole body shudder in sudden heated delight at his touch. Knew, with dismay, that he would have recognised that too.

He said quietly, 'Laura, I have a house overlooking the sea near Sorrento. It is quiet, and very beautiful, and we could be there together in just a few hours.' His dark eyes met hers. 'So— are you still quite sure it is—no?' he asked.

Somehow, even at this stage, she had to retrieve the situation. Somehow...

She stepped back, out of range, lifting her chin in belated defiance. 'I'm—absolutely certain.' Fiercely, she jerked her strap back into place. 'And you—you—you have no right—no right at all to think—to assume...'

'I assume nothing, *carissima*.' He raised his hands in pretended surrender, his tone amused—rueful. 'But you cannot blame me for trying.'

'But I do blame you,' she flung back at him. 'And so would Paolo, if I decided to make trouble and tell him.' She swallowed. 'Do you think he'd be pleased to know you were—going behind his back like this?'

He shrugged. 'Paolo's feelings were never a consideration, I confess. I was far more concerned with my own pleasure, *bella mia*.' He smiled. 'And with yours,' he added softly.

She felt betraying colour swamp her face, but stood her ground. 'You still seem very sure of yourself, *signore*. I find that extraordinary.'

'Losing a battle,' he said, 'does not always alter the course of the war.' He paused. 'And you called me Alessio just now— while you were waiting for me to kiss you.'

Her flush deepened at this all-too-accurate assessment. She said through gritted teeth, 'The war, as you call it, is over. I shall tell Paolo I want to go back to England immediately. As soon as my flight can be rearranged.'

'And he may even agree,' he said. 'As long as it does not

interfere with his own plans. But if there are difficulties, do not hesitate to ask for my help.' He added silkily, 'I have some influence with the airline.'

Ignoring her outraged gasp, he walked across to his lounger, picked up the towel and began to dry himself with total unconcern. Laura snatched up her own things and headed for the steps.

'*Arrivederci.*' His voice followed her. 'Until later, *bellissima.*'

'Until hell freezes over,' she threw back breathlessly, over her shoulder, then forced her shaking legs to carry her up the steps and out of the sight and sound of him.

Alessio watched her go, caught between exultancy and irritation, with a heaped measure of sexual frustration thrown in.

He ached, he thought sombrely, like a moonstruck adolescent.

Stretching out on the lounger, he gazed up at the sky, questions rotating in his mind.

Why, in the name of God, had he let her walk away like that? He'd felt her trembling when he'd touched her. Why hadn't he pressed home his advantage—thrown the cushions on the ground, and drawn her down there with him, peeling the damp swimsuit from her body, and silencing her protests with kisses as he'd taken her, swiftly and simply?

Winning her as his woman, he thought, while he appeased the hunger that was tearing him apart.

Afterwards, he would have sent her to pack her things while he enjoyed another kind of satisfaction—the moment when he told Paolo, and his damnable mother, that he was taking Laura away with him. His mission accomplished in the best possible way.

Then, off to Sorrento to make plans—but for what? The rest of their lives? He frowned swiftly. He had never thought of any woman in those terms. But certainly the weeks to follow—maybe even the months.

At some point, they would have to return to Rome. It would be best, he decided, if he rented an apartment for her. A place without resonances, containing a bed that he'd shared with no one else.

But what was the point of thinking like this, he derided himself, when none of it had happened? When she'd rejected him, using Paolo's name like a shield, as she always did. And he'd let her go...

Dio, he could still taste the cool silkiness of her skin.

And now she wished to leave altogether—to go back to London. Well, so she might, and the sooner the better. Because he would follow.

In England, he could pursue her on his own terms, he thought. He'd have the freedom to date and spoil her exactly as he wished, until her resistance crumbled. And there would be no Zia Lucrezia to poison the well.

Yes, he thought with a sigh of anticipation. London was the perfect answer.

Unless... He sat up suddenly, mind and body reeling as if he'd been punched in the gut. Was it—could it be possible that he'd misjudged the situation completely? Might it be that she was genuinely in love with his weasel of a cousin after all? The idea made him nauseous.

Yet she'd wanted him very badly to kiss her. His experience with women left him in no doubt about that, while her own female instinct must have told her that, once she was in his arms, it would not stop at kissing.

She'd allowed Paolo to kiss her, of course, and all the other intimacies he dared not even contemplate, because they filled him with such blind, impotent rage that he longed to go up to the house, take his cousin from his sick bed, and put him in hospital instead.

He looked down at the book beside him, his mouth hardening. Ah, Francesco, he thought. Was that the image that haunted you every night—your Laura in her husband's arms?

He supposed in some twisted way he should be grateful to his aunt for persuading her malingering son that he was far more sick than he really was, and keeping the lovers apart. At least he didn't have the torment of knowing they were together under his roof.

Santa Madonna, he thought. Anyone might think I was jealous. But I have never been so in my whole life.

And I do not propose to start now, he added grimly.

No, he thought. He would not accept that Laura had any serious feelings for Paolo. Women in love carried their own protection like a heat-shield. No one existed in their private radiant universe but the beloved. Yet he'd been able to feel her awareness of him just as surely as if she'd put out her hand and touched his body.

So, maybe she really believed that, with Paolo, she would be marrying money—or at least where money was. The thought made him wince, but it now had to be faced and dealt with. Because it was clear that, living in one room and working in a bar, she was struggling near the bottom of the ladder.

And, if he was right, he thought cynically, then he would have to convince her that he would be a far more generous proposition than his cousin. That, financially, she would do much better as his mistress than as Paolo's wife.

A much pleasanter task, he resolved, would be to set himself to create for her such an intensity of physical delight that she would forget all other men in his arms. It occurred to him, wryly, that it was the least she deserved.

But what do I deserve? he asked himself quietly. And could find no answer.

'What is this? What are you saying?' Paolo's face was mottled with annoyance.

'I want to go home,' Laura repeated levelly. 'I—I'm totally in the way here, and it's becoming a serious embarrassment for me.'

'An embarrassment for which you will be well paid,' he snapped. He paused. 'But what you ask is not possible. My mother will become suspicious if you go home alone—think that we have quarrelled.'

'I fail to see how,' Laura said coldly. 'We haven't spent enough time together to have a row.'

He waved an impatient hand. 'I have worked too hard to convince her to fail now.' He thought for a moment. 'But we could leave earlier than planned, if we go together—in two or three days, perhaps.'

'Will you be well enough to travel?' Laura asked acidly, but her sarcasm was wasted.

He shrugged. 'We must hope. And *Mamma* intends me to take a little trip with her very soon, so we shall see.'

She said quietly, 'Paolo, I'm deadly serious about this, and I don't intend to wait indefinitely. In twenty-four hours, I'm looking for another flight.'

I can survive that long, she thought bleakly as she went to her room to change for dinner. But this time, I'll be the one adopting the avoidance tactics.

CHAPTER EIGHT

NOTHING happened. Nothing happened. The words echoed and re-echoed in Laura's head, matching the reluctant click of her heels on the tiled floor as she walked to the *salotto* that evening.

But even if that was true, she could hardly take credit for it, she acknowledged bitterly. Nor could she pretend otherwise for her own peace of mind. And she felt as guilty as if she and Paolo had been genuinely involved with each other.

She'd stayed in her room as long as possible, pacing restlessly up and down, frankly dreading the moment when she would have to face Alessio again.

She still seemed to feel his touch as if it were somehow ingrained in her. She'd been almost surprised, as she'd stood under the shower, not to find the actual marks of his fingers—the scar left by the graze of his lips on her skin.

But, invisible or not, they were there, she knew, and she would carry them for ever.

Guillermo was hovering almost anxiously in the hallway, emphasising how late she'd left her arrival, and he sprang forward, beaming, to open the carved double doors to admit her to the *salotto*.

She squared her shoulders and walked in, braced—for what? Mockery—indifference? Or something infinitely more dangerous...

And halted, her brows lifting in astonishment. Because she was not to be alone with Alessio as she'd feared after all. Paolo was there, reclining on a sofa, looking sullen, while the Signora occupied a high-backed armchair nearby, her lips compressed as if annoyed about something.

And, alone by the open windows, looking out into the night, was Alessio, glass in hand.

All heads turned as Laura came forward, and she was immediately aware of an odd atmosphere in the silent room—a kind of angry tension. But she ignored it and went straight to Paolo, who rose sulkily to his feet at her approach.

'Darling,' she said. She reached up and kissed his cheek. 'You didn't say you were getting up for dinner. What a wonderful surprise.'

'Well, I shall not be able to take the time I need to recuperate, when you are in such a hurry to fly home,' he returned peevishly, making her long to kick him.

'Signorina Mason—at last you join us.' The Signora's smile glittered coldly at her. 'We were just talking about you. We have a small predicament, you understand.'

'I can't see what that could be. Paolo's well again.' Laura slid a hand through his arm as she faced the older woman, chin up. 'That's all that really matters.'

'Then I hope you are prepared to be gracious,' said the Signora, her smile a little fixed. 'Because tomorrow I must tear him away from you. We are to pay a visit to my dearest friend, and remain for lunch. She is not aware of your presence here, so I regret that you have not been included in her invitation. You will, I hope, forgive our absence.'

She turned her head towards Alessio, who looked back, his face expressionless.

'And now it seems that you will also be deserted by our host,' she went on, her voice faintly metallic. 'My nephew tells me he has business in Perugia tomorrow that cannot be postponed. We were—discussing the problem.'

Laura found herself torn between relief and a sense of desolation so profound that she was ashamed of herself. She dared not risk a glance in the direction of the tall young man standing in silence by the window.

Once again, it seemed, he was—letting her go.

'It's kind of you to be concerned, *signora*,' she returned with total insincerity. 'But I'm quite accustomed to my own company. Besides, His Excellency has already given me far too much of his time. And I have my packing to do. The time will pass in a flash.'

The Signora gave her a long look, then addressed herself to her nephew. 'Camilla tells me that her son, Fabrizio, will be joining us tomorrow, with his beautiful wife—I forget her name. Do you wish me to convey any message to them on your behalf?'

There was another tingling silence. Then: 'No,' Alessio said icily. 'I thank you.'

'Then let us dine,' said the Signora. 'I have quite an appetite. Come, *signorina*.'

On the way to the dining room, Alessio detained his cousin. 'Why in the name of God have you agreed to go to Trasimeno tomorrow?' he demanded in an undertone.

Paolo shrugged. '*Mamma* has suddenly become more amenable on the subject of my marriage plans. I felt she deserved a small concession. Besides,' he added, leering, 'you heard her say that tasty little plum Vittoria Montecorvo was going to be there. I thought I might try my chances with her.'

A single spark of unholy joy penetrated Alessio's inner darkness. 'Why not?' he drawled. 'Rumour says the lady is—receptive.' He paused. 'Although there is an obstacle, of course.'

'Obstacle?' Paolo stared at him, then laughed. 'You mean the husband? No problem there. He's a total fool.'

'I was thinking,' Alessio said levelly, 'of Signorina Mason.'

'Ah—yes.' Paolo looked shifty. 'But we are not married yet, and a man should be allowed his bachelor pleasures.'

'I could not agree more,' Alessio told him softly. 'I wish you luck, cousin.'

If Laura had thought the presence of other people at the table would make the situation easier, she soon realised her mistake.

Only the Signora, who seemed to have belatedly rediscovered the laws of hospitality and chattered almost vivaciously throughout dinner, appeared to enjoy the lengthy meal. Paolo was lost in some pleasant day-dream and hardly said a word, while Alessio's responses to his aunt's heavily playful remarks were crisp and monosyllabic.

Altogether, the atmosphere was tricky, and Laura, to her shame, found herself remembering almost nostalgically the meals she'd eaten alone with Alessio.

Don't even go there, she adjured herself severely as the ordeal drew to a close.

They returned to the *salotto* for coffee, and it occurred to her that she ought to talk to Paolo privately, and make certain that he'd taken seriously her insistence on going home. And that he intended to call the airline and change their flight as soon as he got back tomorrow.

She said with feigned brightness, 'Paolo, darling, why don't we have our coffee on the terrace? It's such a beautiful night and we can—enjoy the moonlight together.'

For a moment, she thought he was going to refuse, then comprehension dawned. 'But of course,' he said. 'What a wonderful idea.'

As she walked out through the windows she was aware of Alessio's enigmatic stare following her. She paused, realising that she was breathing much too fast, and went to lean on the balustrade as she tried to regain her composure.

If she was honest, she thought, looking up at the sky, it was far from being a lovely night. The air was hot and stifling, and there was a haze over the moon. Wasn't that supposed to be a sign of bad weather to come?

Then, as she waited she heard somewhere in the distance the long-drawn-out howl of an animal, an eerie sound that echoed round the hills, and made the fine hairs stand up on the nape of her neck.

Gasping, she turned and almost cannoned into Alessio, who was standing just behind her.

She recoiled violently. 'Oh, God, you startled me.' She swallowed. 'That noise—did you hear it?'

'It was a wolf, nothing more.' He put the cup of coffee he was carrying on the balustrade. 'They live in the forests, which is one of the reasons Fredo likes to stay up there too—to protect his goats. Didn't Paolo warn you about them?'

'Yes,' she said. 'He mentioned them.' She added coldly, 'But he failed to tell me that they don't all live in forests.'

Alessio winced elaborately. 'A little unjust, *bella mia*. According to the experts, wolves mate for life.'

'The four-legged kind, maybe.' She paused. 'I've never heard any of them before this evening. Why is that?'

'They are more vocal in the early spring, when they are breeding,' he explained. 'Perhaps, tonight, something has disturbed them.'

'Perhaps.' She looked past him towards the lights of the *salotto*. 'Where's Paolo?'

'His mother decided that the night air would be bad for his chest,' he said solemnly. 'And, as they have a journey tomorrow, she has persuaded him to have an early night.' He indicated the cup. 'So I brought your coffee to you.' He added, silkily, 'I regret your disappointment.'

'Paolo's health,' she said stonily, 'is far more important.'

The howl of the wolf came again, and she shivered. 'That's such a—lonely sound.'

'Maybe he is alone, and lonely.' Alessio faced her, leaning against the balustrade. 'A wolf occasionally does separate from the pack, and find that he does not wish to be solitary after all.'

'Well, I won't waste too much sympathy.' Laura kept her tone crisp. 'Wolves are predators, and I expect there are quite enough stray females about to prevent them becoming totally isolated. What do you think, *signore*?'

He grinned at her, unfazed. 'I think that I would very much like to put you across my knee, and spank you, *signorina*,' he drawled. 'But that, alas, would not be—politically correct. So I will leave you before you draw any more unflattering comparisons.'

And that, Laura thought bleakly, when he'd gone and she was left staring into the darkness, was probably our last exchange. I insulted him, and he threatened me with physical violence. Tomorrow he'll be in Perugia. The day after, I'll be on the plane to London. End of story.

And she looked up at the blurred moon, and realised unhappily that she felt like howling herself.

Laura made sure she was around in the morning to bid Paolo an openly fond farewell.

'As soon as you get back,' she whispered as she hugged him, 'you must phone the airline and change our flights. Please, Paolo. I—I can't stand it here much longer.'

'You are better off here than lunching with Camilla Montecorvo. She is a bigger dragon than my mother,' he returned morosely. 'And at least you will have the place to yourself while my cousin is in Perugia on this mysterious business of his.' He gave her a knowing look. 'If you ask me, he has a woman there, so he may not come back at all.' Then, more loudly, 'Arrivederci, carissima. Hold me in your heart until I return.'

Breakfast, as usual, was served on the terrace, although Laura was not so sure this was a good idea. It was not a pleasant morning. The air was sultry, and there was no faint breeze to counteract it. Looking up, she saw that there were small clouds already gathering around the crests of the hills, and realised that Fredo's change in the weather was really on its way.

She thought, Everything's changing... and shivered.

She also noticed that two places had been set at the table.

'His Excellency comes soon,' Emilia told her. 'He swims.'

Yes, thought Laura, biting her lip, fighting the sudden image in her mind. He—told me.

For a moment she let herself wonder what would happen if she went down to the pool and joined him there.

'I've come for my swimming lesson,' she could say as she slid down into the water, and into his arms...

She shook herself mentally. She would never behave in such a way, not in a thousand years, so it was crazy even to think like that. And futile too.

A woman in Perugia, Paolo had said.

The lone wolf off hunting his prey, she thought. Looking for a mate.

And that, she told herself forcibly, her mind flinching, was definitely a no-go area. How the Count Ramontella chose to amuse himself was his own affair. And at least she had ensured that she would not be providing his entertainment, however shamefully tempting that might be.

At that moment Alessio arrived, striding up the steps from the pool, damp hair gleaming and a towel flung over his bare shoulder. He was even wearing, she saw, the same ancient white shorts as on the day of her arrival.

'*Buon giorno.*' He took the seat opposite, the dark gaze scanning her mockingly. 'You did not join me in the pool this morning.'

'I hardly think you expected me to,' Laura retorted coolly, refusing to think about how close a call it had been.

'I expect very little,' he said. 'In that way I am sometimes pleasantly surprised.' His eyes sharpened a little. 'I hope you slept well, but it does not seem so. You have shadows under your eyes.'

'I'm fine,' she said shortly, helping herself to orange juice. 'But I think the heat's beginning to get to me. I'll be glad to go home.'

'Yet for Paolo, this is home,' he reminded her softly. 'So maybe you should try to accustom yourself to our climate, hmm?'

She glanced back at the hills. 'At the moment it seems a little unpredictable.'

'Not at all,' he said. 'We are undoubtedly going to have a storm.' He poured himself some coffee. 'Are you afraid of thunder, Laura *mia*?'

'No, I don't think so.' She looked down at her plate. 'And sometimes a storm can—clear the air.'

'Or breed more storms.' He paused. 'Did you say a fond goodbye to your *innamorato* this morning?'

'He's going for lunch with friends,' she said. 'Not trekking in the Himalayas.'

'Both can be equally dangerous. I suspect that my aunt may have arranged for Beatrice Manzone to be present.' He paused. 'Does that disturb you?'

She kept her eyes fixed on her plate. 'Paolo is old enough to make his own decisions. I—I simply have to trust him to do that.'

'How admirable you are, *mia cara.*' His tone was sardonic. He finished his coffee in a single swallow, and rose. 'And now I too must leave you. But, unlike Paolo, you are in safe hands.' He gave her a tight-lipped smile. 'Guillermo and Emilia will look after you well.'

But when are you coming back? She thought it, but did not say it. Could not say it.

She watched him disappear into the house, and pushed her food away untouched as pain twisted inside her. There was so much, she thought, that she dared not let him see. So much that would still haunt her even when the width of Europe divided them—and when she herself was long forgotten.

It was going to be, she told herself unhappily, a very long day.

In fact, it seemed endless. She didn't even have Caio's company, as the Signora had chosen to reclaim him that morning, announcing imperiously that he would be accompanying them to Trasimeno. Laura had seen him struggling, his small face woebegone as he was carried inexorably to the car.

She spent some time by the pool, but soon gave it up as a bad job. The clouds had begun to gather in earnest, accompanied now by a strong, gusting wind, and even a few spots of rain, so she gathered up her things and returned to the villa.

She'd finished *Mansfield Park* so she went along to Alessio's library and returned it, borrowing *Pride and Prejudice* instead. She knew the story so well, she thought, that she could easily read it before it was time for her to leave.

She lingered for a while looking round the room. It seemed to vibrate with his presence. Any moment now, she thought, he would stride in, flinging himself into the high-backed leather chair behind the desk, and pulling the laptop computer towards him, the dark face absorbed.

The desk itself was immaculately tidy. Besides the laptop, it held only a tray containing a few sheets of the Arleschi Bank's

headed notepaper, and that leather-bound copy of Petrarch's poetry that he'd been reading.

She opened the book at random, and tried to decipher some
of the lines, but it was hopeless—rather like the love the poems
described, she told herself wryly.

From the eyes to the heart, she thought, the words echoing
sadly in her mind. How simple—and how fatal.

To Emilia's obvious concern, she opted to lunch only on soup
and a salad. The working girl's diet, she reminded herself, her
mouth twisting.

Elizabeth Bennett's clashes with Mr Darcy kept her occupied
during the afternoon, but as evening approached Laura began to
get restive. The skies were dark now, the menacing clouds like
slate, and Emilia came bustling in to light the lamps, and also,
she saw, with faint alarm, to bring in some branched candlesticks,
which were placed strategically round the room, while Guillermo
arrived with a basket of logs and proceeded to kindle a fire in
the grate.

Laura was grateful for that, because the temperature had
dropped quite significantly, and the crackling flames made the
room feel cheerful.

But as time passed her worries deepened. Paolo knew she was
relying on him to organise their departure, she thought, so surely
he must return soon, especially with the deterioration in the
weather.

She could see lightning flashes, and hear thunder rumbling
round the hills, coming closer all the time. She remembered nervously that, in spite of her brave words at breakfast, she really
didn't like storms at all. And this one looked as if it was going
to be serious stuff.

It was raining heavily by now, the water drumming a ceaseless
tattoo on the terrace outside. She dared not think what the road
from Besavoro would be like, and her feeling of isolation began
to prey on her.

Think about something else, she adjured herself as she went
off to change for dinner, even though it seemed as if she'd be
eating alone. Don't contemplate Alessio driving back from

Perugia in the Jeep, because he almost certainly won't be. He has every excuse now, always supposing he needed one, to stay the night there.

She put on the silver dress and stood for a moment, regarding herself with disfavour. Her wardrobe had been woefully inadequate for the purpose from day one, she thought. And it was only thanks to Emilia's efficient laundry service that she'd managed to survive.

As for this dress—well, she wouldn't care if she never saw it again.

By the time she got back to the *salotto*, the storm was even closer, and the lamps, she saw, were flickering ominously with every lightning flash.

And then, above the noise of the storm, she heard the distant sound of a vehicle, and a moment later Guillermo's voice raised in greeting.

Paolo, she thought with relief. At last. They'd made it.

She was halfway to the doors when they opened and she halted, her heart bumping, a shocked hand going to her throat.

She said hoarsely, 'I—I thought you were in Perugia.'

'I was,' Alessio said. He advanced into the room, rain glistening on his hair, shrugging off the trench coat he was wearing and throwing it carelessly across the back of a chair. 'But I did not think it was right for you to be alone here in these conditions, so I came back.' He gave her a mocking smile. 'You are allowed to be grateful.'

'I'm used to weather,' she returned, lifting her chin. 'In England we have loads of it.' She hesitated. 'I thought—I hoped Paolo had come back.'

He said lightly, 'I fear I have a disappointment for you. The servants took a call from my aunt two hours ago. In view of the weather, they have decided to remain at Trasimeno for the night. Or that is the story. So—you and I are alone, *bella mia*.'

And as he spoke all the lights went off. Laura cried out, and in a stride Alessio was beside her, taking her hands in his, drawing her towards him.

'Scared of the dark, *carissima*?' he asked softly.

'Not usually,' she said shakily. And far more scared of you, *signore*, she whispered under her breath. 'It's just—everything happening at once,' she added on a little gasp, tinglingly conscious of his proximity.

Don't let him know that it matters, she ordered herself sternly. For heaven's sake, act normally. And say something with no personal connotations, if that's possible.

She cleared her throat. 'Does the power always go off when there's a storm?'

'More often than I could wish. We have a generator for back-up at such times, but I prefer to keep it in reserve for real emergencies.' He paused. 'But Emilia does not like to cook with electricity, so at least dinner is safe.'

He let her go almost casually, and walked over to the fireplace, leaving Laura to breathe freely again. He took down a taper from the wide stone shelf above the hearth and lit it at the fire.

As he moved round the room each candle burst into light like a delicate golden blossom, and in spite of her misgivings Laura was charmed into an involuntary sigh of delight.

'You see.' He tossed the remains of the taper into the wide grate and smiled at her. 'Firelight and candle glow. Better, I think, than electricity.'

Not, she thought, aware that she was trembling inside, in these particular circumstances.

She steadied her voice. 'And certainly more in keeping with the age of the villa.'

Alessio inclined his head courteously. 'As you say.' He paused. 'May I get you a drink?'

'Just some mineral water, please.' Keep sane—keep sober.

His brows rose slightly, but he said nothing, bringing her exactly what she'd asked for and pouring a whisky for himself.

Laura sat on the edge of the sofa, gripping the crystal tumbler in one hand and nervously rearranging the folds of her skirt with the other.

Alessio added some more wood to the fire and straightened, dusting his hands. He sent her a considering look under his lashes, noting the tension in every line of her, and realising that he needed to ease the situation a little.

He said quietly, 'Laura, will you make me a promise?'

She looked up, startled, and instantly wary. 'I don't know. It— it would depend on what it was.'

'Nothing too difficult. I wish you to swear that when you are back in London you will go swimming at least once a week. You lack only confidence.'

'I suppose I could manage that,' she said slowly. 'There are some swimming baths quite near where I live.'

'Then there is no problem.' He added casually, 'Get Paolo to go with you.'

'Maybe,' she said, her mouth curving in such unexpected mischief that his heart missed a beat. 'If his health improves.'

He grinned back, shrugging. 'You can always hope, *carissima*.'

It had worked to some extent, he thought. She was no longer clinging to her glass as if it were a lifeline. But that strange intangible barrier that she'd built between them was still there.

Her reticence frankly bewildered him. He had once been forced to listen to Paolo's drunken boasting about his London conquests, and restraint had never featured as one of the qualities his cousin most favoured in a woman.

So what was he doing with this girl? His Laura, with her level smoky gaze and proud mouth? On her side, he supposed she might have been beguiled initially by Paolo's surface charm, but that must have been seriously eroded by the spoilt-child act of the past week.

And there was another factor that had been gnawing at him too. When he'd gone to post her cards that morning in Besavoro, he'd quickly noted down the names and addresses of the recipients, deciding they might prove useful for future reference. So who was the man Carl that she'd written to at Harman Grace, and what was their connection?

Could this whole trip with Paolo be simply a ploy to make her real lover jealous—provoke him into commitment, maybe? Was this what she was hiding behind that veil of cool containment?

No, he thought. I don't believe that—not in my heart. There's something else. And I have the whole night to find out what it is. To bring down the barrier and possess her utterly.

But first, he thought, he would have to get her to relax—to respond to him—to enjoy being teased a little. Perhaps tease him in return...

After all, he told himself with sudden cynicism, she would not be the first girl in the world to be coaxed into bed with laughter.

For one strange moment, he wished it were all over, and that she were joyously and passionately his, sitting beside him in the Jeep as they set off to some destination where his aunt's malice could not follow. Somewhere they could relax in the enjoyment of some mutual pleasure, he thought restlessly.

He longed, he realised, to fall asleep each night with her in his arms, and wake next to her each morning.

He wanted her as unequivocally and completely as he needed food and clothing. And he was going to wipe from his mind every vestige of the sordid bargain he'd been originally forced into by his aunt. From the moment he'd seen Laura, it had counted for nothing anyway.

But it could have been very different, he reminded himself grimly, so his amazing fortune was hardly deserved. And for a moment the thought made him disturbed and uneasy. And, he realised, almost fearful.

Pulling himself together, he picked up the nearest branch of candles and walked over to her, holding out his hand. 'Let us go into dinner,' he invited quietly.

Laura had made up her mind to plead a headache and go to her room directly after she'd eaten. But it was clearly ridiculous to express a wish for peace and quiet while the storm was still raging overhead, and might prompt Alessio to draw his own conclusions about her sudden need for seclusion. And that could be dangerous.

It was a strange meal. Conversation was necessarily sporadic. The flicker of the candles sent shadows dancing in the corners of the room, until they were eclipsed by the lightning flashes that illumined everything with a weird bluish glow. It seemed to Laura as if each crash of thunder was rolling without pause into the next, and it was difficult to concentrate on Emilia's delicious food when she was constantly jumping out of her skin. It was much easier, in fact, to drink the red wine that Alessio was pouring into her glass, and which made her feel marginally less nervous.

One particular thunderclap, however, seemed to go on for ever, with a long, rumbling roar that made the whole house shake.

Laura put down her spoon. 'Is—is that what an earthquake feels like?' she asked uneasily.

'Almost.' Alessio was frowning, but his gaze softened as he studied her small, pale face. 'My poor Laura,' he said. 'You came here expecting long, hot days and moonlit romantic nights, and instead—the storm of the century. But this house has withstood many storms, if that is any consolation. And it will survive this one too.'

'Yes,' she said. 'Yes, of course.' She bit her lip. 'But—I—I'm quite glad you decided not to stay in Perugia, *signore*.'

'Why, *mia bella*,' he said mockingly. 'What a confession. And I am also—pleased.'

She hesitated. 'Do you think it's this bad at Lake Trasimeno? They will be able to get back tomorrow? Paolo and I have all our travel arrangements to work out.'

He shrugged. 'As to that, I think we must—wait and see.'

'Maybe you could phone—and find out.' She tried not to sound as if she was pleading.

'Why, yes,' he said. 'If the telephone was still working. Guillermo tells me it went off not long after my aunt's call.'

'Oh, God.' She stared at him, unable to hide her shock and dismay. 'But you must have a cell phone, surely.'

'I have more than one, but there is no signal here. I regard that as one of the many pleasures of this house,' Alessio said, pouring more wine.

Lightning filled the room, and he smiled at her, his face a stranger's in the eerie light. 'So, for the time being, we are quite cut off, *mia cara*.' He paused. 'And there is nothing we can do about it,' he added softly.

CHAPTER NINE

THE fierce riot of the storm seemed suddenly to fade to some strange distance, leaving behind a silence that was almost tangible, and twice as scary.

Laura swallowed. 'Cut off?' she echoed. 'But we can't be.'

He shrugged again, almost laconically. 'It happens.'

'But how long are we going to be—stuck here like this?' she demanded defensively.

'Until the storm passes, and we can reassess the situation.'

She shook her head in disbelief. 'Don't you even care?'

'Why? There is nothing I can do, *mia cara*.' He smiled at her. 'So, I shall let you be agitated for both of us.'

Well, she could manage that—no problem, Laura thought grimly.

She picked up her glass, and drank again, aware that her hand was shaking, and hoping—praying—that he wouldn't notice in the uncertain light. She said huskily, 'There's the Jeep. We could—drive somewhere—some place with lights and a phone.'

'In this weather, on that road?' he queried softly. 'You are suddenly very brave, *mia bella*. Far braver than myself, I must tell you. So, do you wish me to give you the keys, because I am going nowhere.' He paused. 'You can drive?'

'I've passed my test,' she said guardedly.

His smile widened. 'Then the decision is yours. But you may feel it is safer to remain here.'

There was a silence, then Laura reluctantly nodded.

'*Bene,*' he approved lazily. 'And now I will make a deal with you, Laura *mia*. In the morning, when this weather has cleared, I will drive you anywhere you wish to go, but only if—tonight...' He paused again, deliberately allowing the silence to lengthen between them.

Laura's mouth felt suddenly dry. She said, 'What—what about tonight, *signore*? What are you asking?'

He said quietly, 'That you will again play the piano for me.'

'Play the piano?' Laura was genuinely taken aback. 'You're not serious.'

'I am most serious. You played the first night you were in my house. Why not the last? After all, you are going back to your own country. I may never have the opportunity to listen to you play again.'

Laura looked down at the table. 'I'd have thought that was a positive advantage.'

He clicked his tongue in reproof. 'And that is false modesty, *mia cara*. I have heard you practising each day. And once I found Emilia weeping in the hall, because your playing brought back memories of my mother for her also.'

'Oh, no.' Laura glanced up in dismay. 'Lord, I'm so sorry.'

'No need,' he said. 'They were happy tears. She loved my mother very much.' He rose. 'So, Laura *mia*, you will indulge me?'

Reluctantly, she followed him to the *salotto*, waiting while he carefully positioned more candelabra on top of the piano.

'There,' he said at last. 'Will that do?'

'Well, yes, I suppose...' She sat down at the keyboard, giving him a questioning look. 'What do you want me to play?'

'Something calming, I think.' Alessio sent a wry glance upwards as thunder rumbled ominously once more. 'That piece you have been practising, perhaps.'

'"Clair de Lune"?' She bit her lip. 'I'd almost forgotten it, and it's still not really up to performance standard.'

'But very beautiful,' he returned. He sat down in the corner of a sofa, stretching long legs in front of him. 'So—if you please?'

Swallowing nervously, she let her fingers touch the keys, searching out the first dreamy chords, only too conscious of the silent man, listening, and watching.

But, somehow, as she played her confidence grew with her concentration, and she found herself moving through the passionate middle section with barely a falter into the gentle, almost yearning clarity of the final passage. And silence.

Alessio rose and walked across to the piano, joining her on the long padded stool. He said softly, *'Grazie,'* and took her hand, raising it to his lips. He turned it gently, pressing his mouth to the leaping pulse in her wrist, then kissed the palm of her hand slowly and sensuously.

Her voice was suddenly a thread. 'Please—don't do that?'

He raised his head, the dark eyes smiling into hers. He said, 'I am not allowed to pay homage to your artistry—even when it has conquered the storm?'

The lightning was barely visible now, she realised, and the thunder only a distant growl.

'It—it does seem to have moved away.' She tried to retrieve her hand, and failed. 'Perhaps the electricity will come on again soon.'

'You don't like the candlelight?'

Laura hesitated. 'Oh, yes, but I wouldn't want to read by it, and I was really hoping to finish my book before tomorrow,' she added over-brightly, aware that his fingers were caressing hers, sending little tremors shivering down her spine. It seemed as if she could feel every thread in her dress touching her bare skin.

'Then we will have to think of some other form of entertainment that may be easier on the eyes.' Alessio paused. 'Do you play cards?'

She shrugged. 'The usual family games.'

'And poker?'

'I know the value of the various hands,' she said. 'But that's about all.'

'I could teach you.'

She stared at him. 'But don't you need more people?' she asked. 'Also it's a gambling game, and I—I haven't any money to lose.'

'It is possible to play for other things besides money, *carissima*. And one learns to make use of whatever is available. Sometimes that can be far more enjoyable than playing for mere cash.' He reached out, his fingers deftly detaching one of the small silver spheres on a chain that hung from her ear. He put it down on an ivory piano key, where it flashed in the candle flame. 'You see? Already you have something to stake.'

Strip poker, Laura thought numbly. Dear God, he's suggesting we should play strip poker...

She wrenched her hand away from his. 'Yes,' she said, her voice bitterly cold. 'And, no doubt, I'd have a great deal to lose, too. That's the problem with all your lessons, *signore*. They come at much too high a cost.'

He smiled at her, unruffled. 'How can you price the value of a new experience, *bella mia*?'

'Oh, you have an answer for everything—or you think you do.' She turned fiercely to face him. 'Why do you do this?' she demanded with sudden huskiness. 'Why do you—torment me like this?'

'Do I torment you, *mia cara*?' he countered harshly. One hand swept aside the silky fall of her hair to cup the nape of her neck, his thumb caressing the hollow beneath her ear, sending a sweet shiver along her nerve endings. 'Then why do you continue to deny what you know we both want?'

She could feel the heat rising in her body, the sudden, terrifying scald of yearning between her thighs, and was bitterly ashamed of her own weakness.

'I can't speak for you, *signore*,' she said, her voice shaking, 'but I just want to get out of here. Out of this house—this country—and back to where I belong. And nothing else.'

She paused, her chin lifting defiantly. 'And now that the storm's over, the telephone could be working again.'

He withdrew his hand with a faint sigh, letting one smooth russet strand of her hair slide lingeringly through his fingers. 'I think you are over-optimistic, Laura *mia*,' he told her drily.

'But could you find out for me—please? I really need to know the times of tomorrow's flights.'

He was her host, she thought with a kind of desperation. He couldn't—wouldn't—refuse her request, however stupid he might think it. She'd asked him to check something. Innate courtesy would take him from the room to do so.

And that would be her chance, she told herself feverishly. Because she needed to get away from him on a far more personal level—and tonight. The door to her room had a lock and key, she knew, and the window shutters had that bolt mechanism she'd used once before. She couldn't risk going through the house, of course, because he might intercept her, but she could cut across the gardens, and be safely locked in her room before he even realised she was missing.

Because she could not trust herself to be alone with him any longer. It was as simple and final as that. The necessity to go into his arms and feel his mouth on hers was an agony she had never experienced before. A consuming anguish she had not dreamed could exist.

And she dared not risk him touching her again. Not when the merest brush of his fingers could turn her to flame.

For a moment, she found herself thinking of Steve, and wondering if this was how he'd felt about her.

I hope not, she thought. I hope not with all my heart.

She watched Alessio walk to the door. Heard his footsteps receding, and his voice calling to Guillermo.

And then she ran across the room, tugging at the windows and their shutters to make a gap she could squeeze through.

She knew the route. She must have used it twenty times since her arrival. But always in the daytime. Never at night. And she had not bargained for the absolute darkness outside. The pretty ornamental lamps that dotted the grounds were out of commission, of course, but there wasn't a star showing, or even a faint glimmer of moonlight.

And, because the storm had passed over at last, she'd assumed the rain would have stopped too, but she was wrong. It was like walking into a wall of water, she thought, gasping.

Before she'd gone fifty yards she was completely drenched, her soaked dress clinging like a second skin, her feet slipping in her wet shoes, and her hair hanging in sodden rats' tails round her face.

She tried to peer through the darkness to get her bearings, but she could see nothing. She could only hope that she was going in the right direction—that somewhere ahead of her was the sanctuary she so desperately needed. She wanted to run, but her feet were sliding on the wet grass, and she was afraid of falling.

She was never sure of the precise moment when she realised that she was being followed. That Alessio was coming after her, running silently and surely in pursuit like a lone wolf from the hills.

She stumbled on, gasping, her heart pounding against her ribs, the words, 'No—please—no,' echoing their frantic rhythm in her brain.

But to no avail. He was suddenly beside her, taking her hand in an iron grasp and pulling her along with him as he ran, head bent.

She tried to drag herself free. 'Leave me alone...'

'*Idiota,*' he snarled breathlessly. 'Do you want me to carry you? *Avanti!*'

At last the sodden grass gave way to paving stones, and she saw a dim glow ahead of her and realised they must have reached her courtyard. Alessio dragged back the heavy glass doors, and pushed her inside ahead of him.

There were candles burning here too on the chest of drawers and the night table, and Emilia had also turned down the bed.

Laura stood, head bent, water running down her face and neck, and dripping off the hem of her skirt to form a forlorn puddle on the floor.

Alessio went past her into the bathroom, his sodden shirt adhering to his body like a second skin. He emerged, barefoot, carrying two towels, one of which he threw to her, using the other to rub his face and hair.

Laura stood motionless, the breath still raw in her lungs from that headlong dash. She held the towel against her in numb fingers, watching as he stripped off his shirt and began to dry his chest and arms. Her heart was beating wildly again, but for a very different reason.

He glanced up, and their eyes met. He said harshly, 'Don't just stand there, little fool. You are soaked to the skin, as I am. Take off your dress before you catch pneumonia.'

Her lips moved. 'I—can't...'

Alessio said something impatient and probably obscene under his breath, and walked over to her, his long fingers going swiftly and ruthlessly to work on the sash, which had tightened into a soggy and almost impenetrable knot. When it came free at last, he peeled the silver dress away from her body, and tossed it to the floor.

Laura made a small sound that might have been protest, but he ignored it anyway. He took the towel from her unresisting grasp and began to blot the chill dampness from her skin. Not gently. She gave an involuntary wince, and felt his touch soften a little. His expression, however, did not, even though the scraps of lace she was wearing were hardly a barrier to his dark gaze.

There was no sound in the room except their own ragged breathing. The shadows dancing on the walls seemed to reduce the room to half its size, closing them into the small area of light provided by the candles.

At last, Alessio threw the towel behind him, and stood looking down at her.

'So,' he said quietly. 'What in the name of God, Laura, did you think you were doing?'

'Running away.' Her voice was barely audible.

'Well, that is plain,' he said with sudden harshness. 'So eager to escape me, it seems, that you could not wait until tomorrow. That you were even prepared to risk damaging your health by this folly tonight. But why, Laura? Why did you do this?'

'You—know.'

'If I did,' he said, 'I would not ask. So, tell me.'

If there were words, she could not think of them. If there were arguments, she could not marshal them. There was her body's need roused to the brink of anguish by the rough movement of his hands on her skin as he'd dried her.

And there was candlelight and the waiting bed...

Oh, God, she thought with desperation. I want him so much. I never knew before—never realised that this could ever happen to me. And I—cannot turn back. Not now. I must have—this night.

Her throat was tight as she swallowed. As she lifted her hands and placed them on his shoulders, reaching up on tiptoe to kiss him shyly and rather clumsily on the mouth.

For a heartbeat, he was still, then his arms went round her, pinning her against him with a fierce hunger he made no attempt to disguise. He said her name quietly and huskily, then his lips took hers, exploring the soft, trembling contours with heated, passionate urgency, his heart lifting in exultation.

She was his, he thought, and she had offered herself as he'd once promised she would. Not that it mattered. The only essential was Laura herself—here at last, in his arms, her lips parting for him eagerly as their kisses deepened into sweet, feverish intimacy, allowing him to taste all the inner honey of her mouth.

He began to caress her, his fingers lightly stroking her throat and neck, then sliding the straps of her bra from her slender shoulders, so that when he found and unclipped its tiny hook the little garment simply fell away from her body. He caught his breath as he looked at her, his eyes heavy with desire, then pulled her closer, so that the tips of her small, perfect breasts grazed his bare chest with delicate eroticism.

He recaptured her mouth, burying his soft groan of pleasure in its moist fragrance, teasing her tongue with his as his hands continued their slow quest down her slim body.

When he reached the barrier of her briefs, he eased his fingers inside their lacy band, gently pushing them down from her hips to the floor.

He'd expected to feel her hands on him, discarding what remained of his clothing, wanting to uncover him in her turn, but, to his faint surprise, she made no such attempt. So he allowed himself a hurried moment to strip naked, before lifting her and putting her on the bed.

He followed her down, taking her in his arms, murmuring husky endearments, glorying in the cool enchantment of her quivering body against his.

He kissed her again, his hands cupping her breasts, stroking the nipples gently until they stood erect to his touch, his inward smile tender as he heard her small, startled sigh of pleasure. He bent his head and caressed the hard, rosy peaks with his mouth, the tip of his tongue drawing circles of sweet torment round the puckered flesh.

He was hotly, achingly aroused, but even in the extremity of his desire for her some remaining glimmer of sanity in his reeling mind warned him that, apart from her kisses, her response was more muted. That she still maintained some element of that reserve that had always intrigued him. Was it possible that, even now, when she was naked in his arms, she could be shy of him?

He wanted her to match him in passion—to be equally enraptured. He longed for the incitement of her hands and mouth on his body, which, so far, to his faint bewilderment, she'd withheld.

Was she scared, perhaps, of the moment when all thinking ceased and the last vestiges of control slipped away?

If so, he would have to be careful, because he could not lose her now.

Very gently, he began to kiss her body, caressing every shadowed curve, each smooth plane as the sweet woman-scent of her filled his nose and mouth.

He rested his cheek against her belly as his hand parted her thighs, finding the scalding moisture of her need.

He heard her gasp, her breathing suddenly frantic as her body arched involuntarily towards him in surrender to the sensuous pressure of his fingers. But he would offer her another kind of delight, he thought, smiling, as he bent to pleasure her with his mouth.

Yet suddenly she was no longer yielding. She was tense—even struggling a little, her hands tangling in his hair, trying to push him away.

'No—no—please.' Her voice was small, stifled. 'You mustn't—I can't...'

'Don't be afraid, *carissima*,' he whispered as he acceded reluctantly to this unexpected resistance. 'I will do nothing you don't like.' Or that I cannot persuade you to like, in time, *mi amore*.

Instead, his fingers sought her tiny hidden bud, stroking it rhythmically—delicately—while his mouth returned to her breast, suckling the engorged peak until she moaned in her throat.

'Touch me,' he breathed, starving for her. He took her hand and carried it to his body, clasping her fingers round his hardness, while he moved over her, positioning himself between her thighs, waiting for her to guide him into her, to surrender to the first deep thrust that would make her his at last.

She was trembling violently, her movements almost awkward as she obeyed his silent demand, taking him to the heated threshold of her womanhood.

But as he began to enter her slowly, gently, prolonging the exquisite moment quite deliberately, he felt the sudden tension in her once again. Realised that the cry of pleasure he'd expected was one of pain instead, and that this time the resistance seemed to be physical.

'*Mi amore*—my sweet one,' he whispered urgently. 'Relax for me.'

And then he looked down into the wide frightened eyes, and he knew.

The hurting—the shock of that tearing pain—stopped almost as soon as it had begun. Laura, her fist pressed to her mouth, was aware of Alessio pulling back. Lifting himself away from her altogether.

She turned away too, curling into the foetal position, her startled body shaking uncontrollably.

She closed her eyes, but she couldn't shut out the sound of his harsh breathing as he fought for control. For an approximation of calm. The passing minutes seemed to stretch into eternity as she lay, waiting.

But for what?

Eventually, he said, 'Laura, look at me. Look at me, now.'

He was sitting up in the bed, the edge of the sheet pulled across his loins. His dark face was a stranger's as he looked at her.

He said, his voice flat, 'This was your first time with a man.' It was a statement, not a question, but he added sharply, 'Do not attempt to lie. I want the truth.'

'Yes.' The single word was a sob.

'You did not think to tell me?'

'I didn't know I needed to.' She bent her head wretchedly. 'It never occurred to me that it might—hurt...' She swallowed convulsively. 'I thought I could pretend—so that you wouldn't know that I hadn't—that I'd never...'

He said very wearily, *'Dio mio.'* There was a long silence, then she felt him stir, and braced herself for the inevitable question.

'Paolo,' he said quietly. 'You—and Paolo—you let me—you let everyone think that you were lovers. Why?'

'Paolo and I decided—to travel together. To see how it worked out.' Even now she had to try and keep the secret. 'Oh, God, I'm so sorry.'

'You have nothing to regret.' His voice was expressionless. 'The blame is mine entirely.'

She felt the mattress shift as he moved, looked up quickly to see him standing beside the bed, pulling on his clothes.

'Alessio.' She lifted herself onto her knees, reaching out a hand to him. 'Where are you going?'

'To my own room,' he said. 'Where else?'

'Please don't go,' she whispered. 'Don't leave me.'

'What you ask is impossible.' The back he kept turned to her was rigid, as if it had been forged out of steel.

She touched her tongue to her dry lips. Her voice was ragged. 'Alessio—please. What happened just now doesn't matter. I—I want you.'

'No,' he said. 'It ends here. And it should never have started. I had no right to—touch you.'

'But I gave you that right.'

'Then be glad I have the strength to leave you,' he said.

'Glad?' Laura echoed. 'How can I be—glad?'

'Because one day you will come to be married,' he said, the words torn harshly from his throat. 'And your innocence is a gift you should keep for your husband. He should have the joy of knowing he will be your first and only lover.'

He took a deep raw breath. 'It is far too—precious an offering to be wasted on someone like me.'

'Not just—someone,' she said in anguish. 'You, Alessio. You, and no one else.'

His need for her was a raw, aching wound, but he could not allow himself to weaken now. Because, one day, he needed to be able to forgive himself.

He bent and picked up his damp shirt from the floor, schooling his expression into cynicism.

'Your persistence forces me to be candid,' he drawled as he faced her. 'Forget the high-flown sentiments, *signorina*. The truth is that I was in the mood for a woman tonight, not an inexperienced girl.' He added coolly, 'Please believe that I have neither the time or the patience to teach you what you need to know in order to please me.'

He saw the stricken look in the grey eyes, and knew it was an image that would haunt him for the rest of his days.

He added, 'In the morning, we will deal with your departure. I am sure you have no wish to linger. Goodnight, *signorina*.' He inclined his head with cruel politeness, and left.

She watched the door close behind him, then looked down at herself with a kind of numb horror. It was the worst humiliation of her life—kneeling here naked—offering herself—pleading with a man who'd just made it brutally clear that he no longer desired her.

It had never occurred to her, she thought blankly, that losing her virginity would be anything but simple. She was a twenty-first-century girl, for God's sake, not some Victorian miss. And it seemed to her bewildered mind as if Alessio, in spite of what he'd just said, had been gentle. Yet, it had still hurt her in a way that she'd found it impossible to disguise.

But that, she thought wretchedly, was nothing compared with the aching agony of his subsequent rejection of her, both physically and emotionally. Her body still burned from its unfulfilled arousal.

Worst of all, she had almost, but thankfully not quite, told him, 'I love you.'

And in the morning she was going to have to face him some-now—with this nightmare between them. And she couldn't bear it—she couldn't...

With a little inarticulate cry, she dived under the covers, dragging them up to her throat, her whole body shaking uncontrollably as the first white-hot tears began to spill down her ashen face.

Alessio stood, shoulders slumped, one hand braced against the tiled wall of the shower, and his head bent against the remorseless cascade of cold water.

If he could manage somehow to numb his body, he thought darkly, then maybe he could also subdue his mind. But he knew already that would not be easy.

How many cold showers would it take to erase the memory of her eager mouth, her warm, slim body stretched beneath him in a surrender that should never have been required of her?

How could you not see? he accused himself savagely. You blind, criminal fool. How could you not realise that she was not merely shy, but totally inexperienced, when everything you did—everything she would not allow you to do—told you that more plainly than any words?

But that first sweet, awkward kiss offered of her own volition had wiped everything from his mind but the assuagement of his own need.

He paused and swore at himself. Was he actually daring to blame her, even marginally, when he had manoeuvred and manipulated her to a point when she had been no longer prepared to resist him?

The fact that his sense of honour had forced him to abandon the seduction in no way diminished his feelings of guilt.

He found himself remembering something his father had once said to him just as he'd been emerging from adolescence. 'Like most young men, you will find enough unscrupulous women in the world, Alessio, to cater for your pleasures. So, treat innocent girls with nothing but respect.' He'd added drily, 'Or until your intentions are entirely honourable.'

It had seemed wise advice, and until now he had followed it.

He had simply not dreamed that Laura could be still a virgin. At the same time, he was shamingly aware of a fierce, almost primitive joy to know that she had never given herself to Paolo.

But she did not belong to him either, he reminded himself with a kind of sick desolation. And, after that last act of necessary cruelty, she never would...

With a groan, he slid down the wall to the tiled floor of the shower, resting his forehead on his drawn-up knees, letting the water beat at him. He had done the right thing, he told himself. He had to believe that.

Yet, he had ignored his father's other piece of worldly wisdom, he realised with a flash of weary cynicism—that a gentleman should never leave the lady in his bed unsatisfied.

Well, his punishment and his penance would be to drive her to Rome tomorrow, and watch her walk away from him at the airport, through the baggage check and passport control, and out of his life.

'Laura,' he whispered. 'My Laura.' He had not cried since his father's funeral, but suddenly, at the sound of her name, he could taste tears, hot and acrid in his throat, and it took every scrap of control he possessed to stop him weeping like a child for his loss.

Swallowing, he lifted himself to his feet and turned off the shower. It was time to pull his life together, he commanded himself grimly, deciding, among other things, how he should deal with his aunt on her return. And, if she made good her threats, how he should handle the aftermath of her revelations.

I should have stood up to her at the start, he thought, his mouth tightening in cold anger as he reached for a towel. Told her to do her worst, then dismissed her from my life, together with Paolo.

But that I can still do, and I will.

It is the wrong that I have done Laura that can never be put right. And somehow I have to live with that for the rest of my days.

CHAPTER TEN

SHE'D cried herself to sleep, but Laura still found no rest. She spent the remainder of a troubled night, tossing and turning in the wide bed, looking for some sort of peace, but finding only wretchedness.

Alessio's hand on her shoulder, shaking her, and his voice telling her curtly to wake up just seemed part of another bad dream, until she opened unwilling eyes and saw him there, standing over her in the pallid daylight.

She snatched at the disarranged covers, dragging them almost frantically to the base of her throat, and saw a dark flush tinge his cheekbones and his mouth tighten to hardness as he registered what she was doing.

He was fully dressed, wearing jeans and a black polo shirt, but, as one swift glance under her lashes revealed, he was also unshaven and heavy-eyed, as if he too had found sleep elusive.

'What—what do you want?' She kept her voice as brusque as his own.

'There has been a serious problem,' he said. 'That noise we heard last night was, in fact, a landslip. Guillermo tried to get down to Besavoro earlier, and found the road to the valley completely blocked with rocks, trees and mud.'

'Blocked?' Laura repeated, her heart missing a beat. 'You mean—we can't get out?'

'Unfortunately, no.' He shrugged. 'But the emergency generator is now working, so you will have hot water, and electric light, which should make your stay more comfortable.'

'But how long am I to be kept here? I—I must get to the airport...'

'Heavy lifting equipment has been requested from Perugia,'

he told her expressionlessly, 'but it may not arrive until tomorrow at the earliest.'

'Not until then?' She digested the news with dismay. 'And how long will it take to clear the road after that?'

Alessio shrugged again. 'Who knows?'

'You don't seem very concerned that we're practically imprisoned here,' she accused, her voice unsteady.

'I regret the inconvenience,' he said icily, 'but at the moment I find Fredo a much greater worry. He is missing, and it is thought that his hut was in the path of the landslide.' He paused. 'I am going down to give what help I can.'

She bit her lip. 'I see—of course.' And as he turned away: 'Alessio, I—I'm really sorry.'

'Why?' At the door, he halted. The backward glance he sent her was unreadable. 'You do not know him.'

'No, but he's your friend, and he obviously means a great deal to you.' She added swiftly, 'I'd be sorry for anyone under the circumstances.' She hesitated. 'Is there anything I can do?'

His smile was faint and brief. 'Perhaps—if you know how to pray.' And was gone.

She lay, staring across the room at the closed door, her instinctive, 'Please take care,' still trembling, unspoken, on her lips. And quite rightly so, she told herself. To have indicated in any way that his well-being mattered to her would be dangerous madness.

So—it had happened, she thought. She had seen him, spoken to him, and somehow survived. She supposed the fact that he'd come to tell her there was an emergency had eased their meeting to a certain extent. It had had a purpose and an urgency that an embarrassed encounter across the breakfast table would have lacked.

But it also meant that she'd been deprived of her only shred of comfort in the entire situation—the knowledge that she was leaving. That she would not have to spend time alone with him, or pass another night in the vain pursuit of sleep under his roof.

All she wanted, quite simply, was to go far away, and try to forget the appalling humiliation of the past twelve hours. If that was, indeed, possible.

Yet now the trap had closed on her again, and she was caught. And there was literally nothing she could do about it except— endure.

It was a very small consolation to know that he would be equally reluctant to have her around after last night's wretched debacle.

Somehow, she reflected painfully, she must have given the impression that she possessed a level of sophistication that was beyond her. A willing female body ready to provide Alessio with the level of entertainment he expected from his sexual partners. Discarded when he realised the truth.

She would carry the stark cruelty of that for the rest of her life, like a scar, she thought.

She turned onto her stomach, burying her face in the pillow. So, when she'd opened her eyes just now and seen him there beside the bed, how was it possible that her body had stirred for one infinitesimal moment in hope and desire?

Because it had done so, she admitted painfully. It might be pathetic and shameful, but it was also quite undeniable.

Which meant that, even now, and in spite of everything, she— wanted him.

Dear God, she thought in angry self-derision, had the totality of his rejection taught her nothing?

Yet it might have been even worse if he'd persuaded her to go away with him. Made what amounted to a public statement of his desire for her, and then, almost in the next breath, dismissed her. At least, hidden away here at the Villa Diana, no one else would know of her humiliation.

She sat up, with sudden determination, pushing her hair back from her face. If she continued thinking along those lines, she could end up feeling grateful to him. And she wasn't.

But lying here, brooding, was no answer either. She had to get up and prepare for the rest of her life. Something that never had included Alessio Ramontella, and never would.

Somehow, she had to put this brief madness behind her, and become sane again.

And I can, she promised herself, lifting her chin with renewed pride. I can, and I will.

It was a strange day. The sky was still heavy with cloud, revealing the sun only in fitful bursts, yet at the same time it was stiflingly hot. The heavy air was filled with the almost jungle smell of wet earth and vegetation, and, although Guillermo had gone down and patiently cleaned out the pool, Laura was not tempted to spend much time out of doors.

In spite of her brave resolution, she found herself prowling round the house, restless and ill-at-ease, as if she were a caged animal.

Alessio did not return, and when Guillermo came back from taking midday food and wine down to those trying to clear some part of the landslide he could only say that Fredo had not yet been found, and the search was continuing.

She wanted to ask, 'Is the Count all right?' but bit back the words. This was not a question she had any reason or any right to ask.

She read the rest of her book and returned it, but did not allow herself to choose another, although *Emma* tempted her. On the one hand, she didn't want to think she might be around long enough to finish it. On the other, she hated the idea of leaving it half unread.

She spent some of her time exploring the house in greater detail, especially the older parts, examining the restoration work that had taken place on frescoed walls and painted ceilings. With a building of this age, careful renovation would always be needed, she thought. A labour of love that would last a lifetime.

And she could understand its attraction. The remoteness that aggravated Paolo had an appeal all its own. She could see how Alessio would regard it as a sanctuary—a much-needed retreat. What she couldn't figure so well was why someone, so very much of the world, should require such a place. Why he should ever want to escape.

But then the entire way the Count conducted his life was an enigma, she thought, or as far as she was concerned anyway. A mystery that had already caused her too much unhappiness, and which she could not afford to probe.

I have to begin to forget, she told herself. However hard that is. However long it takes.

As always, music was her solace. She had no idea when, if ever, she would have access to such a wonderful piano, but she was determined to make the most of it.

She found the book of Beethoven sonatas again, and glanced through them looking for those she'd learned to play in her younger days. She realised for the first time that there was an inscription inside the collection's embossed cover, and that even she could translate this brief message—'To my dearest Valentina from the husband who adores her. My love now and for ever.'

She turned the page swiftly, feeling with embarrassment that she should not have read the message—that she had somehow intruded on something private and precious.

She chose a page number totally at random, and, after loosening up with a few preliminary scales, began to practise.

It was only Emilia's quiet entry with another batch of candles that alerted her to the passage of time since she'd first sat down to play.

'Heavens.' Laura looked almost guiltily at her watch. 'It's nearly time to change for dinner. I didn't realise.' She paused. 'Has—has His Excellency come back yet?'

Emilia pursed her lips. 'No, *signorina*. But do not concern yourself,' she added encouragingly. 'He will return to you very soon.'

Laura was infuriated to find she was blushing again, and hotly, too. 'I just meant that we should maybe—hold dinner until he arrives.'

'But of course, *signorina*.' Emilia's smile was serene but also openly sceptical. Pull the other one, it seemed to advise drily. We are not blind, or deaf, Guillermo and I, and we have known Count Alessio all his life. So you cannot fool us—either of you.

But this time you're wrong, Laura wanted passionately to tell her. And I'm the one who was fooled.

Instead, she bent her head and concentrated on the passage she'd just stumbled over.

Alessio came home half an hour later, walking straight into the *salotto*. Laura glanced up, her hands stilling on the keys as she looked at him. His face was grey with weariness, and his clothes were heavily stained with mud and damp.

She swallowed. 'Did—did you find Fredo?'

'*Sì, alla fine.*' He walked to the drinks table and poured himself a whisky. 'We traced him because his dog was beside him barking.'

She gasped. 'Keeping the wolves away?' she asked huskily.

'Perhaps. It is all too possible.' He drank deeply, then brushed his knuckles across his mouth. 'Fredo is now in hospital, with a badly broken leg.' The words were hoarse and staccato. 'But he was also out all night, lying in that storm, and that is regarded as far more serious. Luca is with him, but his father has not yet regained consciousness.'

He did not tell her of the nightmare journey made by the search party, carrying the badly injured old man on an improvised stretcher across the side of the mountain unaffected by the landslide to the place on the road where the ambulance was waiting.

Nor did he say that the mental image of her face had gone with him every step of the way. That the sight of her now filled him with an illicit joy he could neither excuse nor condone.

Her voice was quiet. 'You said—we could try prayer.'

He walked slowly back and stood by the empty hearth, staring ahead of him. 'I have,' he said. 'I went to the church in Besavoro, and lit a candle.' His smile was twisted. 'I have not done that for a long time.'

As she looked at him Laura caught her breath. 'Your hands—they're bleeding.'

His own downward glance was indifferent. 'It is not important.'

'But you need to take care of them,' Laura insisted. 'Those cuts could easily become infected...'

Her voice tailed away as his brows lifted coldly.

'Your concern is touching, but unnecessary,' he said. 'I can look after myself.'

He spoke more brusquely than he'd intended, because he was fighting an impulse to go and kneel beside her, burying his face in her lap. He saw her flinch at his tone, and cursed himself savagely under his breath.

Yet it was for her own protection, he thought grimly. He dared not soften. He could not take the risk of going near her, or allow himself even the fleeting luxury of touch.

He finished the whisky and set down the glass. 'I had better bathe and change quickly,' he said, striving for a lighter tone. 'No storm will be as bad as Emilia's mood if her dinner is spoiled.'

Laura watched him go, then made her way slowly to her own room. She showered quickly, but made no attempt to dress afterwards. Instead, she sat on the edge of the bed in her cotton robe, staring into space, a prey to her own unhappy thoughts.

She was aroused from her reverie by a tap on the door, and Guillermo's voice telling her that dinner was served.

She got up quickly, and opened the door a fraction. 'I'm not very hungry tonight, Guillermo,' she said. 'I—I think it's the weather. It's so sultry. Will you—explain to His Excellency, please?'

Guillermo's face said plainly that he would prefer not to, and that his wife might also wish to know the reason for the *signorina* being absent, but he gave a small bow of reluctant acquiescence and departed.

But a few minutes later he was knocking again, and this time he presented her with a folded sheet of paper.

The words it contained were terse. 'Laura—do not force me to fetch you.' And it was signed 'Ramontella'.

'*Scusi, signorina.*' Guillermo spread his hands apologetically. 'I tried.'

'Yes,' she said. 'I'm sure you did. Tell the *signore* that I'll be there presently.'

The silver dress was out of bounds, and probably ruined anyway. She was sick of the sight of the blue shift, so she dressed almost defiantly in one of the few outfits she hadn't worn before—a pair of sage-green linen trousers, and a sage and white striped blouse, which buttoned severely to the throat.

Last night's rain hadn't done the pewter sandals any favours either, but they were all she had, so she slipped her feet into them and set off mutinously for the dining room.

Alessio was leaning on the back of his chair, waiting for her.

She lifted her chin, and met his gaze without flinching. She was trying to play it cool, but inside she was melting—dying. The day's wear and tear had been showered away, and, apart from a dressing on one hand, he looked his lean, dangerous self again.

He was wearing the usual black trousers and snowy shirt, and another of those amazing waistcoats—this time in black and gold.

Alessio's own first thought was that if she'd dressed deliberately to disguise her femininity, she had seriously miscalculated. The cut of the linen trousers only accentuated the slight curve of her hips and the length of her slim legs, while the wide waistband reduced her midriff to a hand's span. As he would have had pleasure in proving under different circumstances, he thought with a pang of longing.

And now that he had seen her naked, the prim lines of that blouse were nothing more than a tease. An incitement to remember the delicate beauty beneath.

He felt his heart thud suddenly and unevenly, and snatched at his control, straightening unsmilingly as she walked to the table and sat down.

'Prayer is one thing,' he said softly as she unfolded her napkin. 'Fasting, however, is quite unnecessary.'

She gave him a defiant look. 'I'm just not hungry.'

He shrugged as he took his own seat. 'And I do not care to eat alone,' he retorted. 'Besides, when the food arrives, your appetite will soon return.'

'Is that an order?' she inquired in a dulcet tone.

'No,' he said. 'Merely a prediction.'

She bit her lip, knowing that an icicle had more chance in hell than she had of turning up her nose at Emilia's cooking. 'I notice we're dining by candlelight again.'

'There is not much fuel for the generator,' Alessio returned casually. 'Guillermo wishes to conserve what is left.' His smile was swift and hard. 'Be assured it is not a prelude to romance, *signorina*.'

She met his gaze squarely. 'I never imagined it would be, *signore*.'

'But I understand that work to restore the electricity supply has already begun,' he went on. 'Also the telephones.'

'And the road?'

'I am promised that digging will commence at first light. As soon as there is a way through, you will be on your way to Rome. Does that content you?'

'Yes,' she said quietly. 'Of course.'

'*Bene,*' he commented sardonically. There was a silence, while his dark eyes dwelled on her thoughtfully, before he added, 'Believe me, *signorina*, I am doing all I can to hasten your departure.'

Laura stared down at the polished table. 'Yes,' she said, 'I do—believe it.' She swallowed past the sudden constriction in her throat. 'And I'm—sorry that you're being put to all this trouble, *signore*. I realise, of course, that I—I should never have come here.'

'Well, we can agree on that at least,' Alessio said with a touch of grimness. She thought she was being sent away for all the wrong reasons, he told himself painfully. But how could he possibly explain that he was, for once in his life, trying to do the right thing?

He could not, so maybe it was better to let matters rest as they were. To allow her to go away hurt and hating him—just as long as she did not turn to Paolo instead. The very idea sent a knife twisting inside him.

He found himself trying to hope that she would wait instead for someone decent and honourable who would treat her gently, and with tenderness, when the time came. But he knew that was sheer hypocrisy. That the thought of his Laura in any other man's arms was intolerable anguish, and would always be so.

It was a largely silent meal. Both of them, locked into their own unhappiness, ate just enough of her delicious food to appease Emilia, but without any real relish.

Afterwards, they went to the *salotto* for coffee, but more for convention's sake than a desire to endure more awkward time in each other's company. There were altogether too many no-go areas to avoid, and they both knew it.

Alessio, physically and mentally exhausted by the events of the past twelve hours, was tortured by his longing to have the right to go with Laura to her room, crawl into bed beside her and sleep the clock round in the comfort of her arms.

For her part, Laura felt as if she were suspended in some wretched limbo, waiting for a death sentence to be carried out, but not knowing when the blow might fall.

Everything that occurred tonight—each word, each action—might well be for the last time, she thought, and the knowledge that she would soon go from here and never see him again was almost destroying her.

I can't leave like this, she thought suddenly. Not when, even now, I want him so terribly. I know I don't have the experience he wants, but surely there must be something—*something*—I can do to capture his interest...

'May I offer you something with your coffee?' His tone was coolly formal, and Laura looked up with a start.

'Thank you,' she said. 'May I have *grappa*?'

His brows lifted. 'If that is what you wish.' He paused. 'I did not think you cared for it.'

Dutch courage, Laura thought, but did not say so.

'I certainly found it a shock the first time,' she said with assumed calm. 'But I'd like to—try again. If I may.'

Their eyes met in an odd tingling silence, then Alessio turned away abruptly, and went to the drinks table, returning with two glasses of the colourless spirit.

He handed her one and raised the other, his mouth twisting slightly. *'Salute.'*

She repeated the toast, and drank, hoping that her eyes wouldn't water or her nose bleed. That was hardly the impression she wanted to make.

She was sitting on one of the sofas, but Alessio had gone back to stand by the fireplace, she noticed—which was about as far away as it was possible to get without leaving the room. It was not a promising beginning.

Taking a deep breath, she swallowed the remainder of the *grappa* and held out her empty glass, trying for nonchalance. 'I think I'm developing a taste for this.'

'I do not advise it.' His tone was dry.

'It's my last night in Italy.' Her glance held a faint challenge. 'Maybe I should take a risk or two.'

His mouth tightened, but he refilled her glass without comment and brought it back to her.

As he turned away she said, 'Alessio...'

He looked down at her, frowning slightly. '*Cosa c'e?* What's the matter?'

'Last night, you asked me for a favour,' she said. 'You wanted me to play the piano for you.'

'I have not forgotten.'

'I was thinking that tonight it's my turn—to ask you for something.'

His sudden wariness was almost tangible.

'I am sorry to disappoint you,' he said with cool courtesy. 'But I do not, alas, play the piano.'

'No,' she said, feeling the swift thud of her heart against her ribcage. 'But you do play poker—and you offered to teach me—if you remember.' She took a breath. 'I would like to—take you up on that offer—please.'

He was very still. 'Yet, as you yourself pointed out, *signorina*, a poker school requires more people, and you have no money to lose. Nothing has changed.'

She said softly, 'Except I think you had a very different version in mind.' She detached one of her earrings and held it out to him on the palm of her hand. 'Isn't that so?'

'Perhaps.' The dark face looked as if it had been carved from stone, and his voice was as austere as an arctic wasteland. 'But it was a disgraceful—an unforgivable suggestion, which it shames me to think of, and I must ask you to forget that it was ever made. Also to excuse me. I wish you goodnight, *signorina*.'

He made her a slight, curt bow, and made to move away. She caught at the crisp sleeve of his shirt, detaining him, all pride gone, swept away by the starkness of her need.

Her voice was low, and shook a little. 'Alessio—please. Don't leave me. You—you made me think you wanted me. Wasn't it true?'

'Yes,' he said harshly. 'Or, true then, certainly. But—situations change, and now I wish you to go back to your own country, and get on with your life, as I must continue with mine. Tell yourself that you were never here—that this never happened. Forget me, as I shall forget you.' He released himself implacably from the clasp of her fingers.

'I recommend that you get some sleep,' he added, with chilling politeness. 'You have a long journey ahead of you when tomorrow comes.'

'Yes,' she said. 'And I'll make it without fuss—tomorrow. I swear it. I—I'll never even ask to see you again. But—oh, Alessio, won't you please give me—tonight?'

'I cannot do that.' His throat felt raw, and a heavy stone had lodged itself in his chest. 'And one day, Laura *mia*, you will be grateful to me. When you can look into the eyes of the man you love without shame.'

She watched him go, mind and body equally numb.

'The man you love,' she whispered, brokenly. 'The man you love. Is that really what you said to me? Oh, God, Alessio, if you only knew the terrible irony of that.'

And she buried her face in her hands, sitting motionless in the corner of the sofa, unconscious of the passage of time, until, one by one, the candles guttered and burned out.

Somehow, in the small hours, she got herself back to her own room, undressed and crept into bed, pulling the covers over the top of her head as if she wanted to hide from the coming day.

Or at least from the man she'd be forced to share it with. The man to whom she'd humbled herself for nothing.

No, she thought wretchedly. Not for nothing. For love.

Had he guessed? she wondered yet again. Had he realised that even this brief time in his company had been long enough for her to fall hopelessly, desperately in love with him? To build a pathetic fantasy where some kind of happy ending might be possible?

And was it the knowledge that he could break her heart, rather than his discovery of her inexperience, that had made him turn away from her?

He could hardly have expected such an outcome, after all. And it had clearly turned her from an amusing diversion into a potential nuisance.

And no amount of assurances on her part, or pleading, would convince him otherwise. She was now a serious embarrassment and he wanted her gone. That was totally clear.

I must have been mad, she thought, fighting back a dry sob. What part of 'no' did I not understand?

But that was history now. It had to be, whatever inner pain she was suffering. She would deal with that—somehow—when she was safely back in England.

There could not be long to wait. She would be on her way just as soon as a path to accommodate the Jeep was cleared through the debris. He'd told her that.

Now all that remained to her was to behave with as much dignity as she could still muster for the final hours of her stay at the villa.

And maybe Alessio would be merciful too, she thought unhappily, and leave her to her own devices.

Her packing was almost completed by first light. All that remained to go in the case were the robe she was still wearing and her toiletries.

It was going to be another very hot day, so she decided again to travel in the cream cotton dress, once more immaculately laundered by Emilia.

It's as well I'm leaving, she told herself, trying to wring some humour out of the situation. I could get thoroughly spoiled.

She opened the shutters and stepped out into the courtyard. The storm might never have happened, she thought, viewing the unclouded sky. Yet its aftermath still lingered in all kinds of ways.

It was still very early, and she doubted whether anyone else in the house was even stirring.

In the distance, coming to her through the clear air, she thought she could hear the sound of heavy machinery, but perhaps that was just wishful thinking. A longing to be able to leave the past behind and escape.

Except it might already be too late for that.

She felt suddenly very tired—and strangely defeated. She went slowly back into her room and lay down on top of the bed, stretching with a sigh.

After all, she told herself, she needed a sanctuary, and this was as good as any other. Alessio had no reason to come to this part of the house, and would certainly not be seeking her out deliberately, so she could feel relatively safe.

Presently, she would get showered and dressed, she thought, but not yet. Already the warmth of the sun spilling into the room was making her feel drowsy, and perhaps in sleep she might even find the peace that would be denied her in her waking hours.

So, almost gratefully, Laura closed her eyes, and allowed herself to drift away. But before she had taken more than three steps into the golden landscape before her, she became aware of a voice saying, 'Signorina!'

She opened reluctant eyes to find Emilia bending over her. She sat up slowly. 'Is something wrong?'

'No—no,' Emilia assured her. 'But it is time to eat, signorina. Come.'

'I'm fine—really. I—I don't want any breakfast.'

'Breakfast?' The other woman's brows rose almost comically. 'But it is the *seconda colazione* that awaits you, *signorina*.'

'Lunch?' Laura queried in disbelief. This implied she'd been asleep for hours, when she knew she'd only just closed her eyes.

She peered at her watch, and gulped. 'My God, is it really that time already?'

'*Sì—sì.*' Emilia nodded vigorously, her face firm. 'The *signore* ordered that we should not disturb you from your rest, but you cannot sleep all day. You also need food.'

Laura hesitated. 'I—I have to get dressed first.'

'No need, *signorina.*' Emilia allowed herself a conspiratorial twinkle. 'No one here but you,' she added. 'The *signore* is at the *frana* speaking to engineers about how to make the road safe. He told me he will not come back until late, so you may eat in your *vestaglia.*'

'I see.' Laura got up from the bed, shaking out the crumpled skirts of her robe. He was doing her a kindness, she thought, and she should feel thankful, not sick and empty. Or so lonely that she wanted to weep.

If she'd expected some kind of scratch meal because the master of the house was absent, she was soon proved wrong.

A rich chicken broth was followed by pasta, grilled fish, and a thick meaty stew with herbs and beans, and, after the cheese, there was a creamy pudding tasting of blackcurrant.

I won't want another meal for a week, thought Laura, reflecting wryly that Emilia must have heard about airline food.

She guessed that as soon as Alessio returned she would be leaving, and she wanted to be ready. So she used the siesta time to shower and wash her hair. Emilia, beaming, had told her that the electricity had been restored, but Laura still chose to dry her hair in the sun, sitting on the bench in the courtyard. Last time she'd done this, Caio had been here, she thought idly, then stiffened.

Paolo, she thought. Paolo and his awful mother down at Lake Trasimeno. She hadn't given them a single thought. But then she doubted whether either of them had spared much time to consider her plight either.

Whatever, she would have to leave a message with some excuse to explain her abrupt departure alone. Paolo would probably not be pleased, but that couldn't be helped. And she'd probably done enough to convince his mother that the Manzone marriage was a non-starter, so some good might come out of the bleak misery of this ill-starred visit after all.

But three long hours later she was still waiting. She tried to occupy some time at the piano, but was too irritated by her own lack of concentration to continue, so she put the music away, and closed the lid gently. Another goodbye.

She wandered restlessly round the heated stillness of the garden, trying not to look at her watch too often, and failing. She still had no idea what flight she'd be able to catch. Maybe there wouldn't be one until the next day, now, and she would have to spend the night at the airport, but even that could be endured.

Anywhere, she thought with sudden passion. Please, God, anywhere but here. I can't be with him for another night. I can't...

The sun was setting when she at last heard the sound of the Jeep. She'd been curled up in the corner of the sofa, but now she stiffened, sitting upright, her eyes fixed painfully on the open doorway. She heard his footsteps, his voice in a brief exchange with Guillermo.

Then he came into the room and stood looking at her, in silence, a strange intensity in his dark gaze that parched her mouth and made her tremble inwardly.

She found words from somewhere in a voice she barely recognised as hers. 'The road—is it ready now? Can we go?'

'Sì,' he said quietly. 'It is open.'

She touched the tip of her tongue to her dry lips. 'Then—I'd better get—my things.'

He said something soft and violent under his breath, then came to her, his long stride swallowing the distance between them. He took her wrists, pulling her to her feet in one swift, almost angry movement.

Then he bent his head, and kissed her on the mouth with a searing, passionate yearning that made her whole body shake.

'Forgive me.' The words were forced from him hoarsely as he looked deeply, hungrily into her eyes. 'Laura, forgive me, but I cannot live one more hour without you.'

She should stop this now, a small sane voice in her head kept repeating as Alessio kissed her again. Stop it, and step back, out of harm's way. Anything else was madness.

Madness, she thought as coherent thought spun out of control, leaving nothing but this terrifying frenzy in her blood that demanded to be appeased.

Madness, she told herself on a small sobbing breath as she slid her arms round his neck, and let him carry her out of the room.

CHAPTER ELEVEN

THE whole villa seemed hushed, its only sound his footsteps as he strode swiftly with her along the shadowed corridor to his bedroom.

Alessio kicked the door shut behind him, then crossed the vast room, putting Laura down on the canopied bed. For a long moment he looked down at her, then he bent and quite deliberately took the neckline of her dress in both hands, tearing the thin cotton apart like paper.

She gasped, her eyes dilating in sudden uncertainty, and saw his swift, crooked smile.

He said softly, 'Do not be frightened, *carissima*. I have wanted for so long to do that, but now I will be gentle, I promise.'

He released her from the tangle of fabric, tossing it to the floor behind him, before stripping off his own clothing with unhurried purpose. Then, at last, he lay down beside her, framing her face in his hands as he kissed the lingering doubt from her wide startled eyes, then moved down to her mouth, his lips moving almost languorously on hers until he felt the tension leave her, and her slender body relax trustingly into his arms.

He let the kiss deepen, opening her mouth so that his tongue could seek the moist heat of hers, while his fingertips stroked her face and throat, and the vulnerable angles of her slender shoulders, his touch light and almost undemanding. Almost—but not quite.

He felt the growing tumult of her breathing as he began gently to caress her small, eager breasts.

Her rosy nipples were already hard with desire when he freed them from their lace cups, and bent to adore them with his lips and tongue. She gave a tiny whimper, her head moving restlessly from side to side, colour flaring along her cheekbones.

154

Her shaking hands went to his body, seeking his hardness, driven by the harsh flowering of her own need, but Alessio stopped her, clasping her fingers, and raising them swiftly to his lips.

'Not yet, my sweet one,' he whispered. 'It is too soon for us to enjoy each other as lovers should. This time, *mia cara*, these first moments must be for you alone.'

His hands traced a slow golden path down her body, brushing away her last covering as if it had been a cobweb. And where his hands touched, his lips followed, warm and beguiling. Luring her on.

Telling her—promising her that, this time, there would be no turning back. That the passionate covenant of his nakedness against hers would be fulfilled.

Laura's breathing rasped fiercely in her throat as her aroused senses responded with renewed delight to his caresses, to the physical fact of his nearness, and the warmth of his bare skin brushing hers.

His mouth returned to her breasts, suckling them tenderly as his hand slid between her thighs. She gasped a little in mingled excitement and apprehension, remembering that first time, but discovered at once there was to be nothing painful or threatening in this delicate exploration of her most intimate self.

She found herself sinking into a state of almost languid relaxation, aware of nothing but his fingertips moving on her softly and rhythmically at first, then increasing the pressure into a pattern of deliciously intense sensations. His thumb was stroking her tiny silken mound, coaxing it to heated tumescence, while, at the same time, the long, skilful fingers eased their way slowly into her moist inner heat, forcing the breath from her lungs in a sigh of totally voluptuous pleasure.

His lips moved back to hers, kissing her unhurriedly, his tongue stroking hers, thrusting softly into her mouth, mirroring the frankly sensual play of his hands.

Her earlier languor had fled. There were small flames dancing now behind her tightly closed eyelids. She could not hear, or make a sound, her whole being concentrated on this relentless, exquisite build of pleasure that he was creating for her.

Her body was writhing against his touch, begging mutely for some surcease from this incredible, unbearable spiral of delight that had become almost an agony.

She heard a voice she barely recognised as hers crying out hoarsely as he brought her at last to the peak of consummation, and held her there for an endless moment, before releasing her, and allowing the first uncontrollable spasms of rapture to shudder fiercely through her body, devastating her innocence for ever as she confronted, for the first time, her own sexuality, and his power to arouse it.

And as the first harsh glory of her climax softened into quiet ripples of satiation, there were tears on her face.

Alessio kissed the salt drops away, holding her close, soothing her, murmuring endearments in his own language.

At last she murmured huskily, 'You should have warned me.'

'Warned you of what, *carissima*?'

'How you were going to make me feel.'

She felt him quiver with laughter. 'You do not think, *mia bella*, that might have sounded both conceited and presumptuous?'

She buried her own smile in his shoulder. 'Well—maybe—a little.' She hesitated. 'But I don't expect you've had many failures,' she added with a touch of wistfulness.

There was a silence, then he said gently, 'Shall we agree, *mi amore*, to allow the past to remain where it belongs?' He paused, altering his position slightly but significantly, making her gasp soundlessly. 'The immediate future should concern us more.' He slid his hands under her, lifting her slightly towards him. 'Or I think so—don't you?'

His dark eyes were questioning, his faint smile almost quizzical as he looked down at her, and she felt the hardness of him between her thighs, pressing at the entrance to her newly receptive body.

Laura was suddenly aware of a pang of physical desire so strong—so incredible—that she nearly cried out. Suddenly, she knew that she could not allow herself time to think—to become afraid. To doubt her own capacity to absorb all that male size and strength, and return the pleasure he'd gifted to her only moments before.

Instead, she found herself reaching for him, forgetting her instinctive shyness as she caressed the powerfully rigid shaft with fingers that shook a little, making him groan softly, pleadingly. And then, with a total certainty she barely understood, guiding him into her. Surging almost wildly against the initial restraint of his first thrust to welcome him deeply—endlessly. To defy once and for always any discomfort that might still linger for her in this complete union of their bodies.

But this time there was no pain, only the heated, silken glide of him possessing her—filling her completely over and over again.

Making her realise, with shock, as she clung to his sweat-dampened shoulders, her slim hips echoing his own driving rhythm, that her body had not yet finished with its delight.

That his urgency had captured her too, lifting her, all unaware, to some other unguessed-at plane with heart-stopping speed, showing her that the pinnacle of rapture was there, waiting for her if only—if only she could reach...

Then the last remnants of reality splintered, leaving nothing but the primitive agony of pure sensation. And as she moaned aloud in the final extremity she heard Alessio's voice, hoarse and shaken, saying her name as his sated body crumpled against hers in sheer exhaustion.

The warm scented water was like balm on her sensitised skin, at the same time soothing the frank, unexpected ache of her muscles. Laura lay in Alessio's arms in the deep sunken bath, her head pillowed dreamily on his shoulder as his lips caressed the damp silk of her hair.

There was no point, she thought, in trying to rationalise what had just happened between them. It defied reason or coherent thought. It just—was.

And now nothing would ever be the same again. Or, at least, not for her.

For him, she thought with sudden unhappiness, it was probably just routine. Another eager girl to be taught the art of sexual fulfilment by a man who was undoubtedly ardent and generous— but also diabolically experienced.

He said, 'Where have you gone?'

She glanced up at him, startled. 'I don't know what you mean,' she parried.

'A moment ago you were here with me, and happy. But no longer. So what happened?'

'I'm fine.' She sent him a deliberately provocative look under her lashes. 'Perhaps you're better at reading bodies than minds, *signore*.'

But his glance was thoughtful rather than amused. 'And perhaps you do not always tell the whole truth, *signorina*.'

She turned, pressing her lips passionately against the smooth skin of his shoulder. 'Alessio, I am happy. I swear it. I—I never dreamed I could feel like this. Maybe I'm a little—over-whelmed.'

'And maybe you also need food.' He was smiling now as he reached forward to drain the water. 'I think we must forget dinner, *mia bella*, but maybe I can coax Emilia to provide us with a little supper, hmm?'

'Oh, God.' Laura groaned as he helped her out of the bath. 'What is she going to think?'

He grinned. 'That we have the rest of the night to enjoy, *carissima*, and need all our strength. She will feed us well.'

And so she did, although, to Laura's relief, Emilia allowed Alessio, who had gone on his quest wearing only a pair of jeans, to bring the basket of food from the kitchen himself.

Laura, having ruefully examined the ruin of her dress, had put on his discarded shirt. Now she pirouetted self-consciously for his inspection.

'What do you think?'

The dark eyes glinted. 'I think perhaps supper can wait.'

She laughed, and skipped out of range. 'But I'm starving, *signore*. You wouldn't want me to faint.'

He slanted a wicked grin at her. 'Well, not through hunger, certainly.'

The basket contained cold chicken, cheese, red wine and warm olive bread, which they ate and drank outside in the courtyard, while the goddess Diana stared over their heads with her cold, remote smile.

Laura said, 'I don't think she approves of us.'

'According to the old stories, she approved of very little,' Alessio said lazily as he refilled her glass. 'My grandfather originally commissioned the statue, but I think he was disappointed in the result, and I know my parents were planning to have it replaced at some point.'

'Yet they didn't?'

He was silent for a moment. 'They did not have time,' he said eventually, his voice expressionless. 'My mother was killed on the *autostrada* when I was sixteen. A lorry driver fell asleep at the wheel, and his vehicle crashed through the barrier. And my father never recovered from her death. Within the year, he had suffered a fatal heart attack, which his doctors always believed was triggered by his grief.'

'Oh, God.' Laura sat up, staring at him, shocked. 'Oh, I'm so sorry. I shouldn't have said anything...'

He touched her cheek gently. '*Carissima*, I have not been sixteen for a very long time. And I was looked after with infinite kindness by my godfather, the Marchese D'Agnaccio, and his wonderful wife, Arianna, so I was not left to mourn as a lonely orphan.'

Oh, but I think you were, she told him silently. However well you were looked after. And I think, too, that this explains some of the contradictions I sense in you. The way you seem to retreat to some remote fastness where no one can reach you. The emotional equivalent, perhaps, of this house.

He said, 'You have left me again.'

She bent her head. 'I was thinking of my own father. He died of a heart attack too. He'd liquidised all his assets, remortgaged the house to start up an engineering business with an old friend. He came back from a business trip with a full order book to find the place empty, and his partner gone, taking all the money with him. He must have been planning it for ages, because he'd covered his tracks completely. We were going to lose everything, and Dad collapsed on his way to the creditors' meeting.'

Alessio drew her into his arms, and sat with her, his lips resting gently against her hair.

After a while, he said, 'Would you like to sleep a little, *mia cara*?'

She found her eyes suddenly blurred. 'Yes,' she whispered shakily. 'Yes, Alessio, please. That would be good.'

He took her hand and led her back to the shadowed bedroom. Gently he unbuttoned the shirt, and slipped it from her shoulders, then put her into the bed and drew the sheet over her.

As he came to lie beside her Laura turned into his arms, and heard his voice murmuring to her softly, soothingly, in his own language until drowsiness prevailed, and she drifted away into oblivion.

It was very dark—some time in the small hours—when she awoke to his mouth moving gently, persuasively on hers, calling her senses back to life, and her body to renewed desire.

She yielded, sighing in sensuous acceptance as she fitted herself to him, waiting—eager once more to be overwhelmed—to be carried away on the force of his passion.

But he was, she soon discovered, in no hurry to enter her. No hurry at all.

Instead, she found herself shivering—burning in response as his fingertips stroked and tantalised every warm inch of her, awakening needs that, yesterday, she had not known existed.

His lips caressed her breasts, tugging gently on the hardening nipples until she moaned faintly, then kissed their way down her body, until he reached the joining of her thighs to demand a different kind of surrender.

She was beyond protest, unable to resist him as his mouth claimed her, and she experienced the intimate sorcery of his tongue working its dark magic upon her.

The breath sobbed in her throat as her body writhed helplessly beneath him, torn between shame and exaltation.

He was smiling against her skin, saying that she must speak—must tell him what she liked—what she wanted him to do to her. And was it this? And this? And—most of all—this? And as she was swept away into the maelstrom of anguished pleasure he had unleashed for her she heard her own drowning voice whispering an endless, 'Yes.'

It was almost dawn before they'd finally fallen asleep in each other's arms, and the next time Laura opened her eyes it was full morning, and sunlight was pouring through the slats of the shutters. For a moment, she lay still, savouring her memories, then she turned her head to look at the sleeping man beside her. Only the bed was empty.

She sat up bewilderedly in time to see Alessio emerge from the bathroom, pushing a white shirt into the waistband of his jeans.

She said, 'You're dressed,' and was ashamed of the open disappointment in her voice.

He was laughing as he knelt on the bed beside her, and kissed her mouth. 'I have to wear clothes sometimes, *carissima*. People expect it. Besides, I must go out. It seems that Fredo has recovered consciousness, and is asking for me.'

She stretched delicately, watching the sudden flare in the dark eyes as the sheet slipped down from her body. 'Shall I come with you?'

He glanced swiftly, regretfully at his watch. 'Next time, *carissima*. Now I really must go.' His hand tangled in her hair, drawing her head back for another kiss, longer, slower, deeper than the last, and she slid her arm round his neck, holding him to her.

'Stay here, and get some rest,' he told her softly, detaching himself with open reluctance. 'Because you will need it when I return.' He paused. 'I shall tell the servants you are not to be disturbed.'

Laura groaned. 'I don't think I shall ever be able to face them again.'

He grinned at her. 'Ah, but you will, *Madonna*. Now go back to sleep and dream about me, and I will return very soon.' At the door he turned. 'And then we must talk.' He blew her another kiss, and was gone.

She lay quietly for a while. She had never thought much about her body, except as something to be fed and clothed. Had found the physical facts of passion and consummation faintly ludicrous, and the prospect of actually finding herself in bed with a man—submitting to him—as both awkward and embarrassing.

And she'd never imagined herself as anyone's sex object either. She'd always supposed she was too thin, and her breasts were too small, to make her the focus of a man's desire.

And yet in one terrifying, rapturous night all her ideas had been overturned, and her principles swept aside.

She belonged body and soul to Alessio Ramontella. And every nerve ending she possessed, each muscle, and inch of skin, was providing her with a potent reminder of his total mastery. And of how much he had, indeed, desired her.

She realised she was blushing and pushed the sheet away, swinging her legs to the floor. Too late for blushes now—or even to remember her own careful taboos about casual sex. Although those hours of lovemaking could hardly be described as casual.

And, she thought, she didn't regret a thing. How could she?

She quickly straightened the bed, plumping the crumpled pillows and smoothing the covers flat, then wandered into the bathroom to take a long, luxurious shower. As she soaped herself she recalled other hands touching her, sometimes tantalising, sometimes almost reverent, and felt her heartbeat quicken uncontrollably.

I want him here, she thought, pressing a clenched fist against the tiled wall. I want him now.

As she emerged from the shower and reached for a towel she glimpsed herself in one of the many mirrors and paused, all her earlier doubts about her lack of glamour confirmed.

She turned away, sighing. She still had nothing to wear, and frankly she didn't fancy traversing the house to collect a change of clothing from her room, so she borrowed Alessio's black silk robe instead, rolling up the sleeves and tying the sash in a secure double bow round her slender waist.

The faint fragrance of the cologne he used still lingered in the fabric, she discovered with ridiculous pleasure as she stretched out on top of the bed to wait. She could almost pretend that he was here with her, his arms around her.

And the fantasy became even more real if she closed her eyes. She hadn't meant to doze, but the room was warm, the bed soft, and the shower had relaxed her, so the temptation was irresistible.

As she pillowed her cheek on her hand she remembered how Alessio had kissed her awake only a few hours before, and exactly what it had led to. And she wriggled further into the mattress, smiling a little as her eyelids drooped.

It was the sound of the dog barking excitedly that woke her.

Laura propped herself up on an elbow, and stared around her, momentarily disorientated. Caio, she thought, trying to clear her head. Caio in the courtyard outside her room, wanting her to come out and join him. Except he wasn't here—he was at Lake Trasimeno with the Signora. And—this wasn't her room either. It belonged to Alessio.

Just, she thought slowly, just as she did herself.

And, with that nosedive into reality, she suddenly became aware of something else. The sound of women's voices arguing, not far away. One of them was Emilia's. But the other...

Oh, God, Laura thought, transfixed with horror. It's the Signora. She's back. I have to get out of here.

But she was too late. The door was flung wide, and the Signora came stalking into the room, brushing away the volubly protesting Emilia as if she were a troublesome insect.

'So.' She stared at Laura, still huddled on the bed, and her smile was gloating. 'Just as I expected.' She turned. 'Paolo, my poor son, I grieve for you, but you must come and see this slut you brought here. This *puttana* you thought to honour with our name, and who has become yet another of your cousin's whores.'

Paolo followed her into the room, his expression sullen and

inimical. The look he sent Laura was enough to freeze the blood
'Fool,' it said plainly.

'*Sì, Mammina,*' he said curtly. 'You were right about her and
I was wrong. She has totally betrayed me, and now I cannot bear
the sight of her.' He spat the words. 'So, get rid of her. Make
her go.'

I'm still asleep, thought Laura. And this is a nightmare. A bad
one. He couldn't still intend to keep up this ludicrous pretence
surely?

The situation was fast slipping out of control, and somehow
she had to drag it back to reality. It was hard to be dignified
when wearing nothing but a man's robe, several sizes too large
but she had to try, she thought, scrambling off the bed and facing
them both, her head held high.

She said coldly and clearly, 'Paolo, I do not appreciate having
my privacy invaded, or being insulted like this. So, please stop
this nonsense, and tell your mother the truth.'

'And what truth is that, pray?' the Signora enquired.

Laura sent Paolo an equally fulminating glance. 'That your
son and I are not involved with each other—and never have
been.'

'And nor will we ever be,' he flung back at her. 'You faithless
bitch. Do you think I would want my cousin's leavings?'

Laura felt as if she'd been punched in the midriff. She said
'But that's insane—and you know it.'

'I know only that I want you thrown out of this house.' He
turned to his mother. 'Arrange it, *Mammina*. I wish never to see
her again.'

He stalked from the room, slamming the door behind him
Leaving Laura and the Signora looking at each other.

The older woman sent her a grim smile. 'You hear my son
Pack your things, and go. As the matter is urgent, my car will
take you to the airport at Rome.'

Laura swallowed. 'This is not your house, *signora*. You do
not give orders here. And I am going nowhere until Alessio returns.'

'You are over-familiar, *signorina*.' The Signora's tone was ice

'Or do you imagine some sordid romp gives you the right—a nobody from nowhere—to refer to the Count Ramontella by his given name?'

She paused derisively. 'You mentioned the truth just now. So, hear it. I arranged this little comedy, and I am now ending it. Because I have achieved what I set out to do. I have separated you from my son. With the assistance, of course, of my dear nephew.'

There was a silence, then Laura said slowly, 'What—what are you talking about?'

'I am talking about you—and your host.' She snorted. 'You think my nephew would have laid a finger on you of his own free will? No, and no. I simply made it necessary for him to— oblige me. And he has done so.'

Laura was very still. 'I don't know what you mean.'

The Signora laughed. 'But of course not. You did not know— how could you?—that my nephew has been conducting a disreputable affair with a married woman—the worthless wife, unfortunately, of an old friend's son.' She sighed. 'So sad—and potentially so scandalous. But I agreed not to make this shameful episode public if Alessio would, in his turn, use his powers of seduction to win you away from my son.

'At first, he was reluctant. You are not the type to whom he would naturally be drawn, and very much his social inferior. But he decided that his mistress's dubious honour must be protected at all costs.' She picked up Laura's torn dress from the floor, and studied it. 'And it seems that, in the end, he—warmed to his task.'

Her malicious smile raked like rusty nails over Laura's quivering senses. 'He promised me he would send you home with a beautiful memory, *signorina*. I gather that his ability to do so is almost legendary, so I hope he has kept his word.'

'You mean I was—set up?' Even to her own ears, Laura's voice sounded husky—uncertain. 'You're lying.'

'Ask him,' said the Signora. 'If you are still here when he returns.' She gave a delicate yawn. 'I advise you go quickly and spare him the obvious recriminations. They will do no good. Alessio is, and will always be, a law unto himself.

'Besides,' she added, shrugging, 'it is clear he wishes to avoid a confrontation. As you see, when he learned I was returning, he immediately contrived to be absent. He may feel it is wiser to stay away until you have finally departed.'

'He—knew?' The words stuck in her throat.

'But of course. I telephoned earlier.' The older woman sounded mildly surprised. 'I needed him to make sure you would be found in his bed. That was our agreement.'

She nodded. 'Alessio has fulfilled his part of the bargain, and can now resume his liaison with that pretty idiot Vittoria Montecorvo in perfect safety, as long as he is discreet.' She smiled again. 'As you have found, *signorina*, he prefers fools. And variety.'

She added more brusquely, 'Your services are no longer required, *signorina*. You have amused my nephew for a short time, but anything else is only in your imagination.'

Did I imagine it? Laura asked herself numbly. Did I imagine the murmurs and laughter? The peace and sense of belonging? Was it really—just sex all along?

The Signora turned and opened the door. 'So, please go quietly without embarrassing scenes.'

Laura said quietly, 'Do you really think I'd want to stay?' She brushed past the older woman, and walked quickly away down the passage towards her room, stumbling a little on the hem of the robe.

In the courtyard, the goddess Diana still smiled with that chill serenity. But then, thought Laura as the first slash of pain cut into her, she was accustomed to having love torn to pieces in front of her. So this was the place where she truly belonged.

She ran the rest of the way, just making it into the bathroom before she was violently sick, retching into the toilet bowl until the muscles of her empty stomach were screaming at her, and the world was revolving dizzily round her aching head.

Eventually, she managed to drag herself back to her feet, to rinse her mouth and wash her face somehow. The light golden

tan she'd acquired had turned sallow, she thought, wincing at her
reflection, and her eyes looked like hollow pits.

While beating like a drum in her tired brain were the words,
'I have to get out of here. I have to go. Before he comes back.
I have to go.'

Alessio parked the Jeep in front of the villa and sprang out,
humming to himself. He had assured himself that Fredo was going to make a full recovery, then made his excuses and left, intent
on returning as fast as possible to his warm, beautiful girl.

He had felt totally relaxed and serene on the homeward journey, but his mind was clear and sharp as crystal, visualising the
whole shape of his future life laid out in front of him like a
golden map.

He strode into the house and went straight to his room, but it
was empty. He shrugged off his faint disappointment that Laura
was not there, waiting for him, and went in search of her.

As he walked through the hallway Caio advanced out of the
salotto barking aggressively, halting Alessio in his stride. His
brows snapped together as he realised with sharp dismay the
implications of the dog's presence, and, as if on cue, his aunt
appeared in the doorway of the drawing room.

'*Caro*,' she purred. 'I did not expect you back so soon.'

'And I did not expect you at all, Zia Lucrezia.' His tone was
guarded. 'The road has only just opened again.'

'So Guillermo informed me when I telephoned. He seemed to
feel I should not take the risk, but my driver is a good, safe man.'

She paused. 'You will be pleased to hear that our little con-
spiracy was entirely successful. Paolo was cured of his foolish
infatuation as soon as he saw the English girl sprawling half
naked on your bed.' She added brightly, 'And soon, she will be
on her way to the airport and out of our lives for ever. *Bravo*,
nephew. You have done well.'

Alessio had a curious sensation that it was suddenly impossible
to breathe.

He said hoarsely, 'What have you done? What have you said
to my Laura?'

She shrugged a shoulder. 'I simply—enlightened her as to the real reason for her presence here—and for being honoured with your attentions. Did I do wrong?' She smiled maliciously, adding, 'She seemed to accept the situation quite well. No weeping or hysteria. I was—surprised.'

He said on a groan, *'Santa madonna,'* and began to run.

Laura had taken out the clothes to wear to the airport, and put them on the bed. She went back into the bedroom to fetch her toothbrush and wash-bag, and when she emerged Alessio was standing there.

She recoiled instantly, with a little incoherent cry, and saw him flinch.

He said with shaken urgency, 'Laura, *carissima.* You must let me talk to you. Explain.'

'There's really no need, *signore.*' There was a terrible brightness in her voice. 'Your aunt has already told me everything.'

'No,' he said. 'Not everything.'

'Then at least all I needed to know,' she flashed. 'Which is— I got screwed. Several times and in several different senses of the word.'

His head went back. He said icily, 'How dare you describe what happened between us in those terms?'

'Too vulgar for you, my lord?' She dropped a curtsy. 'I do apologise. Blame my social inferiority.'

He drew a deep breath. 'We shall get nowhere like this.'

'I shall get somewhere,' she said. 'Rome airport, to be precise. After which I shall never have to see anyone from your lying, treacherous family again. And that includes you—you utter bastard.'

There was a tingling silence, then Alessio said quietly, 'I do not blame you for being angry with me.'

'Thanks for the gracious admission,' she said. 'And now perhaps you'll go. I have to finish up here, and your aunt's driver is waiting.'

He said curtly, 'My aunt will need her driver herself. She and Paolo are leaving.'

She lifted her chin. 'Your aunt didn't mention it.'

'She does not yet know. If you wish to go to the airport, I will drive you.'

'No.' She almost shouted the word. 'No, you won't, damn you. Can't you understand? I wouldn't go five yards with you. In fact, I don't want to breathe the same air.'

He looked at her wearily. '*Dio*, Laura. You cannot believe what you are saying.'

'Oh, but I do,' she said. 'And I also believe your aunt. Or are you going to deny that you had me brought here so that you could seduce me?'

He bent his head, wretchedly. '*Mia cara*, it may have begun like that, but—'

'But that's how it ended as well,' she cut across him. 'If memory serves. Now, will you please get out of this room?'

'Not until we have talked. Until I can get you to understand...'

'But I do. It's all perfectly clear. You have a mistress who is married. Your aunt threatened to make the affair public. You took me to bed to keep her quiet.' Her glance dropped scorn. 'You really didn't have to go to those lengths, *signore*. If you thought I was dating your loathsome cousin, then you only had to ask me to stop.'

'Laura—listen to me. I—I wanted you.'

'Please don't expect me to be flattered. What was I—your practice round? Keeping you in shape for your married lady?'

'Your memory does not serve you very well,' he said. 'You know it was not like that.'

'My most recent recollection,' she said, 'is being found by that unholy pair in your bedroom, and having to listen to their insults. Because you set me up. Your aunt telephoned you and said she was on her way.'

'I received no such call,' he said. 'And if I had, then you would have left with me.' He paused. 'If you still insist on going to Rome, then Guillermo will take you. But stay with me, *bella mia*, I beg you. Let me try and make amends.'

'There is nothing you can say, or do.' Her throat ached uncontrollably. 'You tricked me, and I shall always hate you for it. I just want to leave—and never see you again.'

There was another dreadful silence, then he said, slowly and carefully, 'Unfortunately, it may not be that simple for either of us. Last night, I failed to protect you as I should have done, a piece of criminal stupidity for which I must ask your forgiveness. However, it is a fact that you could be carrying my child.'

'Well, don't worry too much, *signore*.' Her voice bit. 'If I am, I'll take appropriate action to deal with it—and it won't cost you a red cent. So you can return to your mistress without a backward glance.'

'Vittoria is not my mistress.' His voice rose in exasperation. 'She never was. It was wrong, and I admit that, but it was only a one-night stand—nothing more.'

'And so was I,' she hit back at him. 'They seem to be your speciality, *signore*.' She saw his head jerk back as if she had struck him, and took a steadying breath. 'Now, if you have nothing more to say—no more lame and meaningless excuses—then, perhaps, you'll finally get out of this room, and leave me alone.'

She could feel his anger like a force field, and braced herself for the explosion, but it did not come.

Instead, he looked her over. 'There is one thing.' His tone was almost conversational. 'My robe. I would like it back, if you please.'

'Of course. I'll leave it—'

He held out a hand. 'Now.'

There was a silence. At last she said quietly, 'Please—don't do this.'

His brows lifted. 'What is your objection, *signorina*?' His tone mocked her. 'I am asking for nothing but the return of my property. Or do you wish me to take it from you?'

Her lips silently formed the word 'no'. She undid the double bow, fumbling a little, then took off the robe, which she rolled into a ball and threw at him. It landed at his feet. She stood her ground, making no attempt to cover herself with her hands. Trying to tell herself that it did not matter. That he already knew everything there was to know about her.

On his way to the *salotto*, he was waylaid by an unhappy Emilia. 'I am so sorry, *Excellenza*, but we tried to keep the *signora*, your aunt, away from your room—and the little one—but we could not stop her. Is this why the Signorina Laura has gone away?'

He said gently, 'The blame is mine alone, Emilia. And the *signorina* had her own reasons for wishing to return to England.'

'But she will come back?'

He found he was bracing himself. Avoiding her concerned glance. 'No,' he said. 'I do not think so.'

He found his aunt ensconced on a sofa, glancing through a fashion magazine and drinking coffee.

'Alessio, *caro*.' She barely glanced up. 'Now that our unwanted guest has departed, I thought I might invite Beatrice Manzone and her father here for a short stay.' She smiled smugly. 'She and Paolo seemed to enjoy each other's company at Trasimeno so much. Maybe, even without your intervention, he might have come round to my way of thinking. Yet it was probably better to be safe.'

'I am sure you would think so.' His voice was harsh. 'However, I must decline to entertain any more guests of yours, Zia Lucrezia. Nor do I wish you or your son to spend another night under my roof.'

There was a silence, then she said, 'If this is a joke, Alessio, it is a poor one.'

His gaze was unswerving. 'Believe me, I have never been more serious. I do not wish to have anything more to do with you. Ever.'

'But Paolo and I are your closest living relatives.' There was a shake in her voice. Uncertainty in the look she sent him. 'Your father was my brother.'

He said icily, 'As I am ashamed to acknowledge. And for most of his life, you and he were strangers—at his wish.' He shook his head. 'I should have ordered you to leave my apartment as soon as you mentioned Vittoria,' he added grimly.

'Yet you did not,' she reminded him swiftly. 'You agreed to

my terms, and you carried them out to the letter, because you did not wish your liaison with her to become known.'

'No,' he said, after a pause. 'I did not. But, on reflection, I think I agreed for Fabrizio's sake, rather than hers. He is a fool, but he is a fool in love, and I cannot blame him for that.' His mouth tightened, then he went on levelly, 'Nor does he deserve public humiliation because his wife does not return his affection.' He shrugged. 'One day he may discover the truth about her, but it will not be through me.'

He gave her a cool, hard glance. 'Guillermo is driving Signorina Mason to Rome, so your own driver is free to take you wherever you wish to go. I would be glad if you would leave as soon as possible.'

The controlled, controlling veneer was beginning to crumble. She said, 'I cannot believe you mean this. You are hardly a saint, Alessio, to trouble yourself over the bedding of one stupid English girl.'

'That is enough.' His voice rang harshly through the big room. 'Believe that the matter is closed, and my decision is final.' He made her a swift formal bow. '*Addio*, Zia Lucrezia.'

She called after him, panic in her tone, but he took no notice.

He was in the library, forcing himself to look through his emails in an attempt at normality, when the door opened and Paolo came in.

He said uneasily, '*Mammina* says you have ordered us from the villa. There must be some misunderstanding.'

'No.' Alessio rose and walked round the desk, leaning back against it, arms folded across his chest. 'This is simply a day for departures—for finally severing damaging connections.' He looked icily at Paolo. 'As you yourself have done, cousin.'

'You mean the little Laura?' Paolo shrugged. 'But consider— if I had pretended to forgive her for sleeping with you, *Mammina* would never have believed it. So what else could I do but get rid of her?'

Alessio considered him, his mouth set. 'You do not seem distraught at her loss,' he commented.

'On the contrary, it is damned inconvenient,' Paolo said sourly.

'Until your intervention, I had *Mammina* nicely fooled. Another few days, and she would have admitted defeat over the Manzone girl.'

'How little you know.' Alessio's eyes were coolly watchful. 'And how was Signorina Mason involved in this—foolery?'

Paolo shrugged. 'There's no point in keeping it secret, any longer. The truth is, I picked her up in London. *Mammina* was right about that. Offered her a free holiday, plus cash, if she pretended to be in love with me.'

He gave a lascivious grin. 'I must say she threw herself into the role. Under all that English cool, she was a hot little number—as you must have found out last night.

'But I'm surprised she didn't tell you herself—during pillow talk,' he went on. 'But perhaps you didn't give her time, eh? I've been there myself, cousin, and I'm sure you had much better things for that pretty mouth to do...'

There was a blur of movement, and the odd sensation that he'd collided head-on with a stone pillar.

He found he was lying on the floor, his jaw aching, with Alessio standing over him, flexing his right hand.

He said softly, dangerously, 'That is a filthy lie, and we both know it. You never touched Laura Mason, and you will never speak of her in those terms again.' He paused. 'When you return to London, it will be to clear your desk. You no longer work for the Arleschi Bank. Now get out.'

He strode from the room, leaving Paolo to scramble to his feet, unaided and cursing violently.

'You will be sorry for this, cousin,' he whispered silently, gingerly feeling his jaw as Alessio's tall figure disappeared. 'And so will your little bedmate. Oh, yes, I know how to make her very sorry.'

Laura sat down at her desk and switched on her computer. It was almost a relief to find herself back at work, she thought, sighing. At least it would mean she would have something else to think about—during daylight hours, anyway. At night, it was not so easy to control her thoughts or dreams.

The long drive to the airport had been conducted pretty much in silence, although she'd been aware of Guillermo sending anxious glances in her direction.

Once they'd arrived, he had asked her quietly if she was sure—quite sure—she wished to do this, and she had said yes—yes, she was. And he had taken her to the desk, and arranged to have her ticket transferred to the next available flight in four hours' time. The transaction had taken place in Italian, and she was sure she heard him mention the Count Ramontella's name, but it had seemed wiser not to ask or protest. She was getting out of there, wasn't she? And more easily than she could have hoped?

The actual means had no longer seemed important.

'You have no message for me to take to His Excellency?' His voice was sad as he bade her goodbye.

'No,' she said, past the agonising tightness in her throat. 'No, thank you. Everything necessary has been said.'

On the plane, she pretended to sleep while the events of the past twenty-four hours rolled like a film loop through her weary mind, tormenting her over and over again. Telling her how gullible she'd been. The worst kind of fool.

The time since her return had not been easy for her either. Gaynor had naturally wanted to know why she'd come back earlier than expected, and didn't seem wholly convinced by Laura saying evasively that things hadn't worked out exactly as expected.

Her friend was also astute enough to read the signs of deep trouble behind Laura's attempt at a brave face.

'Please don't tell me you ended up falling for this Paolo after all?' she asked, dismayed.

'God, no.' Laura's voice was vehement with disgust. She'd encountered him briefly just as she'd been leaving the villa, and he'd called her an ugly name and told her she wouldn't get a cent of the money he'd promised. And for a second she'd stared at him, almost dazedly, wondering what he was talking about. Because it had all been such a long time ago, their arrangement, and now everything had changed, so that nothing—nothing mattered any more, least of all money...

'Well, that's a relief.' Gaynor gave her a shrewd glance. 'But, all the same, I'm sure there was someone. And when you want to talk, I'll listen.'

But Laura knew she would never want to discuss Alessio. The pain of his betrayal—of the knowledge that she'd been cynically seduced for the worst of all possible reasons—was too raw and too deep. She simply had to endure, somehow, and wait for time and distance to do their work.

However, at least she knew she wasn't pregnant. She'd had incontrovertible proof of that only two days after her return, and, for a long, bewildered moment, she'd not known whether to be glad or sorry. Just as there'd been times when she'd found herself wondering if he would—come after her...

But that was just a stupid lapse into unforgivable sentimentality, she told herself strongly. And never to be repeated. She wasn't having his baby, and he hadn't followed her to England. So, she'd been fortunate to be spared even more regret—more heartbreak. Nothing else.

And now she had to concentrate on things that really mattered, like her work. Because this was a big day for her. Her trial period at Harman Grace was complete, and she was about to receive her final appraisal and, hopefully, a permanent job offer, which would give her tottering confidence a much-needed boost.

So, she went into Carl's office for her interview with her shoulders back, and a smile nailed on.

But she'd no sooner sat down than he said, 'Laura, I'm afraid I have some bad news.'

She looked at him, startled. 'My appraisal?'

'No, that was good, as always. But, things are a bit tight economically just now, and we're having to make cuts, so there's only one job on offer instead of two as we planned.' His face radiated discomfort. 'And it's been decided to offer it to Bevan instead.'

'Bevan?' Her voice was incredulous. 'But you can't. He's struggled from day one. We've all had to pick up the pieces from his mistakes. Everyone knows that. My God, you know it.'

He did not meet her gaze. 'Nevertheless, it's the decision that's been reached—and I'm personally very sorry to lose you.'

Laura looked down at her hands, clenched together in her lap. She said half to herself, 'This cannot be happening to me. It can't.'

There was a silence, then Carl leaned forward, speaking quietly. 'I should not be telling you this, and it's strictly non-attributable. But the decision came from the top. One of our big new clients has put in some kind of complaint about you. Alleged you were incompetent, and impossible to work with, and that they'd take their business elsewhere unless you were fired. Times are hard, Laura, and the directors decided they couldn't take the risk.'

Laura gasped. 'They didn't even ask me for an explanation? It could be some terrible mistake.'

Carl shook his head. 'I'm afraid not.' His glance was compassionate. 'Some way, and only God knows how, you've managed to make an enemy of the head of the Arleschi Bank, honey. Alessio Ramontella himself. I've actually seen his personal letter to the board. And that's about as bad as it gets. No further explanations necessary.' He paused, saying sharply, 'Laura—are you OK? You look like a ghost.'

She felt like one too, only she knew she couldn't be dead, because she was too hurt, and too angry. It wasn't enough for Alessio to destroy her emotionally, she thought. He'd deliberately set out to ruin her career as well. She supposed it had to be revenge for their last encounter. After all, his anger had been almost tangible. He must have acted at once, to punish her for the things she'd said.

She thought, 'But that's impossible. He doesn't even know I work here,' and only realised she'd spoken aloud when Carl stared at her in disbelief.

'You mean there's something behind all this. You really know this guy?'

She lifted her chin. 'No,' she said quietly and clearly. 'I don't know him, and I never have done. Thankfully, he's a total stranger to me, and that's how he'll remain.' She rose. 'Now, I'll go and clear my desk.'

Alessio glanced at his watch, wondering how soon he could make a discreet exit from the reception. Attendance had been unavoidable, but now his duty was done and he wanted to leave. Not least because the Montecorvos were there, and he had been aware all evening of Vittoria's eyes following him hungrily round the enormous room.

If I'd known, he thought, wild horses wouldn't have dragged me here.

Since his return to Rome, Vittoria's letters and phone calls had returned in full force, although he'd responded to none of them. But she was clearly not giving up without a struggle, he realised, caught between annoyance and resignation.

He was on his way to the door when a slender crimson-tipped hand descended on his arm, and he was assailed by a waft of perfume, expensive and unmistakable.

He halted, groaning silently. 'Vittoria,' he offered insincerely. 'What a pleasure.'

She pouted, standing close to him, offering him a spectacularly indiscreet view of her cleavage. 'How can you say that, *caro mio*, when you know you have been avoiding me? Is it because of your aunt?' She lowered her voice, shuddering. 'She made my visit to Trasimeno a nightmare, the old witch, dropping hints like poison. But now she is no longer in the city. She has moved to her house in Tuscany, and Fabrizio's mother says she has no plans to return. So, we are safe.'

He began, 'Vittoria—' but she interrupted.

'*Caro*, I have good news. A friend of mine has an apartment not far from the Via Veneto, only she has been sent to Paris on business.

'And I have the key. We can meet there, without danger, whenever we wish.'

She smiled up at him, showing him the tip of her tongue between her lips. 'And you do wish it, don't you, *carissimo*? Because you are not seeing anyone else. I know that. Since you came back from Umbria over a month ago, you have been living like a recluse. Everyone says so.'

'Then, I am obliged to everyone for their concern,' he said icily. 'Unlike most of them, I have work to do.'

'But you cannot work all the time, *mi amore*.' Her low voice was insinuating. 'Your body needs exercise as well as your mind. And you cannot have forgotten how good we were together, Alessio *mio*. I shall never forget, and your Vittoria needs you— so badly.'

He met her gleaming, greedy gaze, and, with a sudden jolt of renewed pain, found himself remembering other eyes. Grey eyes that had smiled up at him in trust, then turned smoky with desire, before shining with astonished rapture as her body had yielded up its last sweet secrets. And all for him alone.

All that warmth and joy—and the small wicked giggle that had entranced him—and which it almost broke his heart to re-member.

Laura, he thought with yearning, and sudden passion. Ah, *Dio*, my Laura—my beloved.

And suddenly Alessio knew what he had to do, just as surely as he'd done when he'd driven back to the villa on that last morning, only to find his plans—his entire future—wrecked by the disaster that had been waiting for him.

He took the hand that was still clutching his sleeve, and kissed it briefly and formally.

'You flatter me,' he said with cold civility. 'But I fear it is impossible to accept your charming invitation. You see, I have fallen deeply in love, and I hope very soon to be married. I am sure you understand. Feel free to tell—everyone. So, goodnight, Vittoria—and goodbye.'

And he strode away, leaving her staring after him, with two ugly spots of colour burning in her face.

It had been raining all day, and the air felt cool, promising a hint of autumn to come as Laura arrived back at the house and went slowly upstairs to her room.

She had been suffering from stomach cramps for most of the

evening, and, as the wine bar was quiet, Hattie, the owner, had
dosed her with paracetamol and sent her home early.

She didn't usually have painful periods, but supposed wearily
that her symptoms could be caused by stress. Because she still
hadn't found another agency to take her on. Carl had given her
a good reference, but prospective employers always wanted to
know why she'd left Harman Grace after only three months. And
they did not like the answer they were given.

So she was fortunate that Hattie could offer her full-time wait-
ressing. But the money wasn't good, and there was little to spare
once the rent was paid.

Her room felt damp and cheerless as she let herself in, and
she shivered a little. She decided a shower might be comforting,
but soon discovered that the water was only lukewarm in the
small chilly bathroom. She sighed to herself. It seemed she would
have to settle for the comfort of a hot-water bottle instead. She
put on her elderly flowered cotton pyjamas and her dressing
gown, and trailed off to the kitchen, carrying the rubber bag with
its Winnie the Pooh cover.

She found Gaynor there ahead of her, taking the coffee jar
from the cupboard, the kettle already heating on the stove. She
swung round, starting violently, as Laura came in.

'My God, what are you doing here?'

'I live here.' Laura stared at her. 'Is something wrong?'

'No, no. But you're usually so much later than this. I wondered.'

'It's that time of the month again.' Laura grimaced. 'Hattie let
me finish the shift early.' She held up the hot-water bottle. 'I just
came to fill this.'

'Oh, hell.' Gaynor looked dismayed. 'I mean—what—what a
shame. Poor you.' She gave Laura a smile that on anyone else
would have looked shifty. 'Well, you go ahead. Your need is
greater than mine, so the coffee can wait,' she added, backing to
the door. 'I mean it—really. I—I'll check on you later.'

Laura turned to the stove with a mental shrug. There were two
beakers on the small counter, she noticed, so clearly her friend
had company. But what was there in that to make her so jumpy?

She carefully filled her bottle, and carried it back to her room, pausing first to tap at Gaynor's closed door and call, 'The kitchen's all yours.'

She'd taken two steps into the room before she realised that she was not alone. Or saw who was waiting for her, tall in his elegant charcoal suit, his dark face watchful and unsmiling as he looked at her.

He said quietly, *'Buonasera.'*

She clutched her bottle in front of her as if it were a defensive weapon. 'Good evening be damned,' she said raggedly. 'How did you get in here?'

'Your friend, who took pity on me when she heard me knocking, told me you had returned, and the door was open. So I came in.' He paused. 'It is good to see you again.'

She ignored that. 'What—what the hell are you doing here?' she demanded shakily. 'How did you find me?'

'The postcards you wrote that day in Besavoro, and I mailed for you. They had addresses on them.'

'Of all the devious...' Laura began furiously, then stopped, and took a deep breath. 'What do you want?'

'I want you, Laura.' His voice was quiet. 'I wish you to return with me to Italy.'

She took a step backwards, glaring at him. 'Is that why you had me fired—to offer me alternative work as your mistress?' She lifted her chin. 'I don't regard sharing your bed as a good career move, *signore*. So I suggest you get out of here—and I mean now.'

Alessio's brows lifted. 'Is that what you mean?' he asked with a kind of polite interest. 'Or what you think you should say?'

'Don't play word games,' she hit back fiercely. 'And before you ask, by the way, there's no baby.'

'So I gather.' His tone was rueful. 'Your friend has already informed me I have chosen the wrong time of the month to visit you.'

The hot-water bottle fell to the floor as Laura said hoarsely, 'Gaynor—said that—and to you?' She shook her head. 'Oh, God, I don't believe it. I—I'll kill her.'

For the first time, he smiled faintly. 'Ah, no, I was grateful for the warning, believe me. My friends who are already husbands tell me that sometimes a back rub can help. Would you like me to try?'

She stared at him in outrage, then marched to the door and flung it open. 'I'd like you to go to hell.' Her voice shook. 'Just—leave.'

'Not without you, *carissima*.' Alessio took off his jacket, and tossed it over the back of her armchair, then began to unbutton his waistcoat.

'Stop,' Laura said furiously. 'Stop right there. What do you think you're doing?'

He smiled at her. 'It has been a long and interesting day, and it is not over yet. I thought I would make myself comfortable, *cara mia*.'

'Not,' she said, 'in my flat. And don't call me that.'

'Then what shall I say?' he asked softly. 'My angel, my beautiful one? *Mi adorata*? For you are all these things, Laura *mia*, and more.'

'No.' She wanted to stamp in vexation, but remembered just in time that she was barefoot. 'I hate you. I want you out of my life. I told you so.'

'*Sì*,' he agreed. 'I am not likely to forget.'

'Nor did you,' she threw at him. 'In fact you wrote a stinking letter to Harman Grace, telling them to sack me as a result.'

'A letter was certainly written,' he said. 'I saw it today. But it did not come from me.'

Her jaw dropped. 'You—went to the agency.'

'It was during working hours,' he explained. 'I expected you to be there. I hoped you might be more welcoming when others were present. Instead I spoke to your former boss, who eventually showed me this ridiculous forgery.'

'It was on your notepaper,' Laura said. 'Signed by you. He told me.'

'I replaced my letterheads a few months ago. Those at the villa, I only use as scrap now. Paolo of course would not know this. And his imitation of my signature was a poor one, also.'

She blinked. 'Paolo? Why should he do such a thing?'

'He was angry and wished to revenge himself on me—on us both. And, to an extent, he succeeded.'

'But—he didn't care about me—about what had happened.'

'Ah,' Alessio said softly. 'But he cared very much when I knocked him down.'

She gasped. 'You did that? Why?'

'It is not important,' he said in swift dismissal. 'And his own troubles are mounting rapidly. He now works for Signor Manzone, and I am told his wedding is imminent.'

He paused. 'And you would have had to give up your job in any case, *mi amore*,' he added almost casually. 'You cannot live in Italy and work in London. The commuting would be too difficult.'

She lifted her chin. 'I think you must have lost your mind, Count Ramontella. I have no intention of living in Italy.'

He sighed. 'That makes things difficult. I have already had the statue of Diana removed from the garden, and had drawings commissioned so that we can choose a replacement. Also work has begun on the swimming pool to provide a shallower end until you get more confidence.

'And Caio is inconsolable without you. He howls regularly outside your room. At times, I have considered joining him.'

'Caio?' Laura lifted a dazed hand to her forehead. 'How does he feature in all this? He's your aunt's dog. Is she still at the villa?'

'No,' he said with sudden grimness. 'She is not. She left shortly after you, and I have no wish ever to see her again.

'But Caio did not wish to go in the car when she departed, and bit Paolo, who tried to make him. Then my aunt unwisely intervened, and he bit her too. She announced she was going to have him put down immediately, so Emilia quite rightly rescued him and brought him to me.'

He smiled at her. 'But we all know the one he truly loves.'

She said passionately, 'Stop this—stop it, please. I don't understand. I don't know what's happening. Why you're talking like this.'

He said gently, 'If you closed the door, and sat down, I could explain more easily, I think.'

'I don't want you to explain.' Her voice rose almost to a wail. 'I want you to go. To leave me in peace. It's cruel of you to come here like this. Saying these things.'

'Cruel of me to love you, *carissima*? To wish to make you my wife?'

'Why should you wish to do that, *signore*?' She didn't look at him. 'To make it easier for you to go on with your secret affair with that—that woman?'

He came across to her, detached her unresisting fingers from the handle, and closed the door firmly, leaning against it as he looked down at her.

He said quietly, 'Laura, I did a bad thing, and I cannot defend myself. Nor do I wish to hurt you more than I have done, but I must be honest with you if there is to be any hope for us.

'I am not having an affair with Vittoria Montecorvo. I never was. But we had met several times, and she had let me see she was available. After that our paths seemed to cross many times. I think someone must have hinted to my aunt that this was so, and she decided to have me watched.'

Laura stared up at him. 'Your own aunt would do that?'

He said grimly, 'You have met her. My father told me once that since childhood she had enjoyed observing other people's misdemeanours, and discovering their secrets, so that she could use them to gain unpleasant advantages, like a spider keeping dead flies in a web to enjoy later. Oddly, I never thought she would do it to me.

'Unfortunately, her need for a favour coincided with Vittoria's brief incursion into my life, and as I did not wish to cause the breakdown of Vittoria's marriage, or even see her again after my one indiscretion, it seemed I had no choice but to do as I was required, however distasteful.'

He sighed. 'And then I saw you, Laura, and in that moment everything changed.' He tried to smile. 'Do you remember how Petrarch spoke of his Laura? Because you too went from my eyes straight to my heart, *mi adorata*, and I was lost for ever.

Although I did not realise that immediately,' he added candidly. 'Which is why my original intentions were not strictly honourable.'

'No,' she said in a low voice. 'I—realised that.' Lost for ever, she thought. I felt that too.

He took her hand. Held it.

'You see—I am trying to be truthful,' he said quietly. 'I thought that once you belonged to me that everything would be simple. That I would take you away where my aunt could not reach us, and you would never need to know about that devil's bargain I had made with her. I even told myself it no longer mattered, because I wanted you for myself—and myself alone. And that justified everything. Only, I soon found it did not.

'When I realised—that first time—that you were a virgin, it almost destroyed me. Because I knew that you did not deserve to surrender your innocence for such a reason. That I could not— would not do what my aunt demanded, and to hell with the consequences.'

'Yet you did—eventually.' Her voice was small and strained.

'*Mi amore*, as I told you, I took you only because I could not live without you any longer. And I thought you felt the same.' He looked deeply—questioningly—into her eyes. 'Was I so wrong?'

'No,' she admitted, with reluctance. 'You were—right.'

'I was also certain that news of the landslide would keep my aunt at bay for another twenty-four hours, at least,' he went on. 'And that would give me time.'

'Time for what?'

'To tell you everything, *mia bella*, as I knew I must, if there was to be complete honesty between us. So, I drove back from Besavoro to make my confession, and beg absolution before I asked you to become my wife. But, again, it was too late. Once more, I had underestimated my aunt.

'And when you looked at me—spoke to me as you did—I thought I had placed myself beyond your forgiveness for ever. That, hurting you as I had done, I could hope for nothing. That I had ruined both our lives.'

He took her other hand. Drew her gently towards him. 'Is it true, Laura *mia*? Is all hope gone? Or can you try to forgive me, and let me teach you to love me as I think you were beginning to? As I love you?' His voice sank to a whisper. 'Don't send me away, *carissima*, and make us both wretched. Try to forgive—and let me stay with you tonight.'

She said jerkily, 'But you can't—stay. You know that.'

He sighed, and kissed the top of her head. 'Do you think I am totally devoid of decency or patience, *mi amore*? And do you also intend to turn me out of our bed each month when we are married? I don't think so.' He paused. 'I want to sleep with you, Laura. To take care of you. Nothing more. Don't you want that too?'

'Yes, I suppose—I don't know,' she said with a sob. 'But I still can't let you stay. I just—can't.'

'Why not, my angel?' His voice was tender. 'When it is what we both want.'

There were so many sensible and excellent reasons for sending him away for ever, yet she couldn't think of one of them.

Instead, she heard herself say crossly, 'Because I'm wearing really horrible pyjamas.' And then she burst into tears.

When she calmed down, she found that they had somehow moved to the armchair, and she was sitting curled up on Alessio's lap.

'So,' he said, drying her face with his handkerchief. 'If I promise to buy you something prettier in the morning, may I stay?'

'I can hardly throw you out,' she mumbled into his shoulder.

'And will you marry me as soon as it can be arranged?'

She was silent for a moment. 'How can I?' she asked unhappily. 'We hardly know each other. And I don't belong in your world, Alessio. If I hadn't been forced on your attention, you'd never have given me a second glance.'

'You are my world, Laura,' he said softly. 'Without you, there is nothing. Don't you understand that, my dear one?

'I want yours to be the face I see when I wake each morning. I want to see you smile at me across our dining table. I want to teach you to swim so well that you will dive off the side of our boat with me. I want to be with you when our children are born, and to love you and protect you as long as we both live.'

She said with a little gasp, 'Oh, Alessio—I love you too, so very much. I wanted to stop—I tried hard to—and to hate you—but I—I couldn't. And I've been so lonely—and so terribly unhappy. And I'd marry you tomorrow, if it was possible. Only it isn't. I—I can't just disappear to Italy with you.' Her hands twisted together. 'There's my family to consider. That's why I needed a decent job, so that I could help my mother with my brother's education.'

She swallowed. 'I only agreed to help Paolo because he was going to pay me, but then he didn't.'

'Good,' he said. 'Because I have no wish for you to be obliged to such a creature.' He stroked her hair back from her face. '*Mia cara*, I am going to be your husband, and I shall look after your mother and brother as if they were my own. How could you doubt it?'

'But I don't know that she'll accept that.' Laura's face was troubled. 'She has her fair share of pride.'

'We will go and see her tomorrow,' he said. 'After all, I have to ask her permission to marry you. And I will talk to her—persuade her that it will be my pleasure to care for you all. I am sure she will see reason.'

Laura raised her head from his shoulder, and looked at him in quiet fascination. 'I bet she will at that,' she said, her lips twitching in sudden amusement. 'Are you always going to expect your own way, *signore*, once we're married?'

'Of course,' he said softly, and wickedly, drawing her close again. 'But I will always try to ensure that your way and mine are the same, my sweet one.'

He bent his head and kissed her, his mouth moving on hers with a gentle, almost reverent restraint that made her want to cry again. But she didn't. And they held each other, and kissed again, whispering the words that lovers used. And were happy.

Much later, Laura was sitting up in bed finishing the *tisana* he had made her from Gaynor's herb tea when Alessio came back from the bathroom, her refilled hot-water bottle dangling from his lean fingers.

She looked at him with real compunction. 'Darling, I'm sorry. It's all so—unromantic.'

'Then maybe we should put romance aside for a while,' he said gently. 'And think only about love.'

He undressed quickly, and slid into the narrow bed behind her, wrapping her warmly and closely in his arms. Making her feel relaxed and at peace for the first time in weeks.

She was almost asleep when a thought came to her. 'Alessio,' she whispered drowsily. 'Will you promise me one more thing?'

'Anything, *mia bella*.'

She smiled in the darkness. 'Will you still teach me to play strip poker?'

'It might be arranged,' he returned softly. 'On some winter night, when we are safely married, and the fire is warm and the candles are lit.' He paused. 'But I must warn you, *carissima*. I cheat.'

Laura turned her head and aimed a sleepy kiss at the corner of his mouth.

'So do I, my darling,' she murmured in deep contentment. 'So do I.'

THREE MORE FREE BOOKS!

HARLEQUIN *Presents*

This September, purchase 6 Harlequin Presents books and get these THREE books for FREE!

IN THE BANKER'S BED
by Cathy Williams

CITY CINDERELLA
by Catherine George

AT THE PLAYBOY'S PLEASURE
by Kim Lawrence

To receive the THREE FREE BOOKS above, please send us 6 (six) proofs
of purchase from Harlequin Presents books to the addresses below.

<table>
<tr><td><u>In the U.S.:</u></td><td><u>In Canada:</u></td></tr>
<tr><td>Presents Free Book Offer</td><td>Presents Free Book Offer</td></tr>
<tr><td>P.O. Box 9057</td><td>P.O. Box 622</td></tr>
<tr><td>Buffalo, NY</td><td>Fort Erie, ON</td></tr>
<tr><td>14269-9057</td><td>L2A 5X3</td></tr>
</table>

- -

Name (PLEASE PRINT)

Address   Apt. #

City   State/Prov.   Zip/Postal Code
098 KKL DXJP

To receive your THREE FREE BOOKS (Retail value: $13.50 U.S./$15.75 CAN.)
complete the above form. Mail it to us with 6 (six) proofs of purchase, which
can be found in all Harlequin Presents books in September 2006. Requests
must be postmarked no later than October 31, 2006. Please allow 4–6 weeks
for delivery. Offer valid in Canada and the U.S. only. While quantities last.
Offer limited to one per household.

> **Presents
> Free Book
> Offer**
> PROOF OF
> PURCHASE
> HPPOPSEP06

www.eHarlequin.com